The Black Book

First published in 2018 by

Becomeshakespeare.com

Wordit Content Design & Editing Services Pvt Ltd
Unit - 26, Building A -1, Nr Wadala RTO,
Wadala (East), Mumbai 400037, India
T: +91 8080226699

ISBN - 978-93-88573-09-2

Absolute JERRY

absolutejerry.com

About the author

Absolute JERRY, is a name of a brand that is me. I am my company and I am my foundation. Absolute JERRY is a link to everything I do, Every work I've done and everything I am going to do.

From a pen to a camera, I work my way. The world of my cinema goes by the name **Absolute JERRY Films**. My work is discoverable at YouTube under the same title. But if you truly want to know everything about me then this where you would find me.

absolutejerry.com

Acknowledgments

Thank you Mom for all the support I ever needed. Can never have a person like you in my life.

Thank you Mrunmayi Narnaware for the drawing and designing the Book Cover Art.

To all my silly friends for just being there whenever I needed them.

And to you for being real, Absolute.

About

The Black Book

Blue Umbrella Black Raincoat is the second instalment of the series *The Black Book*. But that doesn't make it a sequel to its predecessor *Kalyan 2 Pune Love Express*. It simply means that both the stories are happening in the same universe and sometimes in the same timeline as well. That being said, the question arises

Do I need to read Kalyan 2 Pune Love Express before reading this book?

Well the answer to that question is, It's all up to you. Neither of the stories are dependent on each other, but yeah, If you want to explore the universe then I suggest you to have a look up there as well,

absolutejerry.com/novels or
kalyan2puneloveexpress.strikingly.com

Or maybe not...

Contents

Contents

Contents

Chapter 1

Blue Umbrella Black Raincoat

Brown eyes, boy-cut hair, peach lip-gloss and tiny diamond earrings on her fair skin, stood a lady, 27, near the six story company with glass facade, iHNS private limited. She was wearing a beige coloured shirt, tight, tucked in her black pant with a cigarette in her right hand and a watch on her left. Standing alone on the footpath she smoked it fearlessly. Figure maintained, but slightly thin because of too much smoking with an average height of 5'5". She smoked holding a blue umbrella under her left arm.

Grey eyes, clean shaved face, a small framed spectacle on an oval, pale brownish face. A man, 29, riding a pulsar 180 motorcycle wearing a black raincoat and a bag. The climate was cloudy, but the rain hasn't started yet. He slowed down his motorcycle as he reached the company, iHNS private limited. Parked it in front of the girl smoking a cigarette, holding the blue umbrella. He removed his raincoat and kept it on top of the petrol tank and started walking away.

Suddenly it started to rain and the girl smoking a cigarette unfolded her blue umbrella. Her cigarette was almost finished, so she threw it away on the road. The moment she threw it, it fell on the left leg of the man running back to his bike.

"I'm really sorry." She said chewing her teeth, but he didn't utter a word and kept walking towards his bike.

"Sir, I'm really sorry for that, it happened by mistake."

She apologized again and he ignored her as he walked by his bike, took his raincoat and flicked it on her face splashing its water at her. Closing her eyes, she faced away pouting her lips, but half of her face and shirt already got wet.

Wearing his raincoat, he walked away. She kept staring him angrily increasing her breath until he left her sight. Then gradually she began walking burning her ego mumbling.

"Son of a bitch."

Getting inside her office she spoke with her assistant and went to her cabin. Manager Deborah D'mello written on her desk where she sat, picking up the phone she said.

"Ok, send them in." And in a few minutes.

"May I come in?" Said the guy pushing the door. But the moment he got in, they both got shocked because he was the guy who splashed water at her earlier and now he is being interviewed by her to work in a company where she is the manager.

"Of course, come in." She said sarcastically and smirked. He looked at her suspiciously closing the door as he got in.

"Keep that raincoat away from me... near the door." She overreacted.

He pulled his feeling of aggression together and slipped it away with a sigh of breath. Walked towards her and sat on the seat in front of her.

"You don't know the manners of an interview, do you?" She said. Biting his lips, he stood up from the chair.

"Good-afternoon, ma'am."

"Good...Afternoon indeed, have a seat." She said then he sat staring down in disgust.

"Introduce yourself." She said, leaning back to her chair. Keeping him straight in her sight with a plastic smile. Nodding his head, in a polite way, he started.

"Myself, Richard Buthello, my age is 29. Recently I was working in Techno Industries but because of some reasons I had to resign..."

"Resigned or fired?" She interrupted. Then after a small pause of stares, he replied.

"Resigned..." He said in a threatening pitch.

"Ok... Continue." She said while he just bowed his head while scratching his chin.

"What happened? Are you nervous and is this your first interview in... 29 years?" She said.

"Eh... I would like to start over" His voice was unpleasantly intense.

"That's unprofessional, so if something happens while working, then you simply can't start over. You need to learn to handle the situation and improve it on the go... Which I don't think you are capable of doing as a Team leader that you came here to work as."

Hearing that Richard stopped the conversation, silently taking his files he stood up and walked near the door. As he was exiting the room, she said.

"Hey... Black... Black raincoat, take that with you."

He took his raincoat and left. The moment the door shut, she chuckled and smiled, raising her left eyebrow.

Afterward, at 4 pm, Deborah left the office driving her car, Škoda superb, to home. On the way, she was stopped by two traffic policemen who asked for her licence. After searching her entire car for 10 minutes, she couldn't find her purse where she keeps it. The policeman fined her 250 bucks which she was unable to pay because all her money was in the purse which was nowhere to be found. And this policeman didn't even fall pray for her looks. As they were both old and unreasonable people taking their job seriously, which made it even worse for her to get out of the situation.

Driving his pulsar on the street, even Richard got stopped by a traffic police. When he turned around, he saw Deborah standing with the policeman in tension holding her blue umbrella. She too looked at him with an ominous look. The police checked his license and let him go. When he was about to start his bike Deborah said.

"Hey... Hi..." And she smiled, but he kept staring her with no emotions on his face.

"I need your help... Buddy." She said raising her left eyebrow.

"Buddy!" He exclaimed and then giggled as he said.

"Do I even know you?" Said innocently with a mixed emotion yet confused expression.

"Richard please, this is not a great time for your jokes..." As she was speaking, he interrupted.

"How do you know my name?" He said and she glared at him. Then he continued, "Oh, you must have seen it on my licence when it was with them."

He said pointing at the policemen. Hearing this, she got shook and stayed that way for a few seconds, then as she started speaking both policemen were looking at Richard.

"Listen, don't kid right now. If you help me now then, I will definitely help you with the stuff at your office which you are having difficulty to ge..."

As she was speaking, again Richard interrupted making an irritated face.

"Hey blue... blue umbrella, don't wink at me. Please don't. I'm not that kind of guy." He said and both policemen shifted their sight quickly to Deborah scaring her off. While they were staring her gossiping with each other, Richard started his bike and before leaving the place he just glanced her, winking he left. While she stood there embarrassed.

He reached home, removed his raincoat and bag and sat on the couch.

"Hey, how was the interview?" His younger brother, 21, asked.

"The interviewer was a bitch." He replied.

"Got it." His brother said nodding.

A few days later, Richard received a letter. He got stunned and confused, waving his hair roughly reading the letter that said: "Dear Richard, you are appointed as a Team leader for the voice processing department at iHNS private limited...."

Chapter 2

Blue Umbrella vs Black Raincoat

Pale yellow lights, crystal themed ceiling, a circular antique styled table that had glasses of wine and an Italian dish chicken Piccata, sat Richard wearing a dark magenta shirt with a shade of black and Van Heusen jeans. He was dining with a lady, light brown eyes perfectly eye lined, with lipstick like the kiss of wine, fair skin with long curly hairs falling down her backless maroon one piece. And heels long enough to match her height with Richard. He picked the glass of wine and stared it, then looked into her eyes, raising the glass at eye level and said.

"I don't know which one is darker, the colour of wine or your lipstick."

"Your future!" She replied chuckling.

"I was going to say your lips then I would've lightened the colour of your lips by kissing them but you spoilt the game."

"Oh! So I'll buy a bottle of wine and we will continue this game at my place." She played with his eyes.

"That's a nice plan, but before that, I've one more plan."

"I'm sure to fail that as well." She teased winking at him. Then he took out a small box out of his pocket. Got down on a knee, hiding both of his hands behind as he expressed.

"I knew the first time I laid my eyes on you, you are something special for me. You are like a candle light whenever there is darkness around me, a missing piece of my jigsaw puzzle, a pearl to my oyster...."

"No..." She interrupted And the whole room laid eyes on them with a sound of shock.

"No?" His voice sounded like a puppy.

"No, no... I mean I won't fail you this time, continue..." She said and the crowd had a sigh of relief.

"Hmm... Eh... I was saying, you are like eh... Mm..." Then he pulled the box out and opened it saying.

"Marina George, Will you marry me?" Showing her a platinum ring with her name carved on it and faint hearts on either side. Yes, Marina George was his girlfriend before and now his fiancé. He bought that ring a long time ago, but because of his unemployment, he didn't move ahead. Apparently, now he is a team leader, ergo, time to settle in life.

Next day, Deborah walked swiftly towards the company as she was running late. Her office was on the 5th floor of the building. She stepped inside and was pacing towards the elevator until she saw Richard in it. Richard too stared her making a wired eye contact. Deborah sauntered facing sideways to the cafeteria lifting her chin up to her attitude and decided to take another elevator. Her breath was easing as the doors of the elevator were shutting but before it shut, Richard kept his hand on the door at the cleft and reopened the elevator. Faking a smile with his lips shut as she entered avoiding eye contact. He was flattering himself as it was making his manager uncomfortable. Throughout the floors, she felt negative vibes in her consciousness. Five floors uplifts felt like fifteen because of over thinking as time tends to pass slowly when we want it to speed up. "5th floor", the door opened and Deborah walked out pouting while Richard walked cherishing. He strolled toward his new cabin as a Team leader. As he was admiring the desk and surrounding, the landline rang and he received an invite at the manager's office.

"Bitch called." He mumbled as he went.

"May I come in?" He asked with a smile.

"Yes, please come in." She replied with an evil smile, eye contact, a signal to a Mexican standoff.

He walked towards the seat and this time he just stood by it, as he clearly remembers how he was insulted before for sitting without permission.

"Very well, have a seat." She said and he sat. Sweeping her short hair above her forehead, she asked.

"So, do you like your new cabin?" She smirked.

"Yes, it is nice" He replied calmly as he hunches that she wants to sniff his excitement.

19

"I won't chat much, just want to say get prepared for what is coming. You are assigned to batch G. They all are freshers and I hope you would be able to teach them. Make them perfect for their calls, we want the best employee from you for this BPO, good luck" She ended slowly in a low pitch, but what she meant was, "good luck, you'll need it."

After two hours of training for team leader by Mr Shree, he was appointed to assist his new team, Batch G. But who were Batch G?

He entered his batch room, all the candidates were sitting in their chair around a big long rectangular white table. He stood in front of the LED screen in the room.

"Good morning all, My name is Richard Butthelo and I'm your new team leader." He introduced himself and started his session.

"Now, Let me tell you about this company. iHNS private limited. We are basically..."

As Richard continued the induction of the company he could easily see the look of bewilderment in his candidates so he stopped and asked.

"Why you all are so confused? Am I going too fast?"

"No, sir. But we already know this company very well."

"It is good, you have done your research well. But still, I would like to inform you everything about this company. See as a team leader it's my job to prepare freshers up to the mark."

"But we are not fresher, this is batch G."

"Batch G? What exactly is batch G?"

Richard asked and one candidate explained everything that Batch G was.

Batch G:

iHNS private limited is a BPO which deals with medical claims of several countries and its branches are situated in India, Dubai, Croatia and Australia. Here are several batches maintained to control various departments. In those batches, the worst one is Batch G. This batch is basically for all those people are unsuitable for other batches because of weak working skills so they are transferred here. A special experienced person is always kept in charge here. But he recently resigned so there was a vacancy and Richard Butthelo got the Job now. The team leader of batch G.

There was a moment of silence as Richard was perplexed because he had no training to tackle the problem of the employees.

"I'll just come back in a minute." He said and left the room. He was on his way to the HR's office, but just before knocking on the door, he felt as if he was losing. A clear suspicion was in his mind that Deborah deliberately made him in charge of a batch he was under qualified so he had to quit with an embarrassment. Well, he certainly wouldn't let that happen. Ergo, he walked back into his room and said.

"Alright Batch G. Let me get you ready to get back to work."

But he wasn't a superhero who could do anything he wants. He did suck at this because to help an employee with a problem you got to be experienced with every single detail of the issue but he himself was a fresher at that company. At last, he went home disappointed and even left Job early which itself was highly unprofessional.

Then, at the end of the day in Deborah's cabinet came a candidate for an interview. Well, not exactly an interview but for the sign in process as she already cleared all the interviews already.

"Come in, have a seat." Deborah said.

"Thank you." She replied.

"You are selected for the position of a financial planner, right?"

"Yes, I am."

"You may start with the induction."

"Ahem... Good evening, ma'am. Myself Idhaya Banerjee. I'm from Pune..."

Chapter 3

HR cabin

Ms.D'mello gazed into the mirror lightening her lips with a Sephora's Huda beauty lip strobe, gold and pink pearls. Then she took the hair brush out and straightened her short hairs above her eyes. Biting her lips, she backed from the mirror, covered in a towel, from her thighs to cleavage and moved towards the closet. Hung her towel on the door and stood naked looking for a dress to wear. Then she kept her feet between a white panty and pulled it up her thighs till the name Calvin Klein was above her ass. Then wore a cream pant over it. Which fitted perfectly, giving sexy shape to her butt. Standing top naked she leant over the lower compartment of the closet and picked up a red bra. Wearing it, she then wore a white shirt from Zara and within a few minutes got ready and left for the job.

At the office, came Richard in a blue shirt and black pant. He walked inside his cabin, they all greeted and sat down, ready to be briefed along with a new employee. She wore a cyan coloured top with black pant, brown skin face with dark black eyes and straight but slightly curly hairs.

"Is this your first day in this batch?"

"Yes." She replied smiling.

"From which batch are you transferred?" Richard asked.

"Actually I'm from Pune, I used to work there earlier and now I got here in Airoli."

He nodded and mumbled. "Hmm... So they send people here all the way from Pune too." Then he asked her.

"What is your name?"

"Idhaya Banerjee." She replied.

"Ok. So now let's start with today's session."

Richard was well prepared this time and he was able to solve everybody's difficulty except Idhaya's.

"What is going on here?" She said after half an hour of confusion.

"What do you mean?" Richard asked.

"I'm not here for any training on improving my calling skills, this shit isn't useful for me." She said out of frustration.

"Idhaya, Your language!" Richard exclaimed.

"I'm sorry for my language, but it's only the result of the pathetic situation going on here. Firstly, I'm a financial planner from a repudiated company 'Wipro', Pune. And I came all the way from Pune to Airoli for a better Job and what am I getting, downgraded..."

After hearing that Richard thought for a few seconds then said. "I guess, a huge misunderstanding happened with the management."

"You guess?" She was being sarcastic.

"Who interviewed you anyway?"

"The manager, Deborah!"

"Deborah? Oh! Of course, there's a misunderstanding then." Richard became quite optimistic about the situation.

"Why? Is she that bad at work that she does it all the time?"

"Not sure about that, but she is bad. You don't worry ma'am. My job is to solve problems, I'm sure I'll help you out too." Richard smiled assuring and he took Idhaya with her at the cabin of HR.

At HR's cabin,

"Yeah, come in?" HR said after Richard knocked on the door.

"I've never seen you both before in this office, you'll be the new recruits, right?"

"Yes, ma'am, I'm Richard Buthello. The new Team leader and she is Idhaya ban...." As he was saying, HR interrupted saying.

"Oh, you are Idhaya Banerjee."

"Yes, ma'am." She smiled.

"She is here for a very special program of one's Croatia. In fact, I myself passed her resume." HR said looking at Richard and continued to Idhaya.

"So how are you liking this new working place."

"Not... very much."

"Why? What's troubling you?"

"Work itself, I'm not doing here what I'm supposed to do. My designation is a financial planner, but instead here I'm put up in a batch of candidates who wants to improve their calling skills. That's nowhere near to my profession."

"Who assigned you to this Job? Him? Richard?" HR asked.

"No, she came into my batch by mistake, batch G." Richard replied.

"Wait, I thought you were new to this company and only permanent team leader are supposed to be running batch G." HR got baffled and disappointed. As she stared both of them for a moment to ask.

"Who appointed both of you?"

And both Richard and Idhaya answered in a sync. "Deborah D'mello."

A few moments later, when they both were sitting outside the cabin, she had a smile of relief while he had a smile of victory. As he was trying to imagine Deborah's unpleasant conversation with HR about how irresponsible she had become with her work. But she didn't know that her irresponsibility was nothing but a sort of personal vendetta.

In a few minutes, Idhaya was called in as Deborah walked out. While she passed by, glancing Richard she spoke as ice.

"Never seen you happy before, never thought I would."

"I'm always an unexpected surprise Mrs Manager."

"It's miss, anyway, it seems like you have started your first move as in taking my pawn out. Let's see how well you play ahead." Deborah said raising her left eyebrow.

"This isn't my first move and the game had already begun the day we met. In fact, I've already taken a few of your pawns before." He smirked.

"That means we are equally numbered, but it's my move now. See you tomorrow at the office." She said glancing away. While he just sat there with mixed feeling.

Chapter 4

Latte

Misty rains stormed over the city, making each and every window of the tallest building in Airoli, Signia Oceans, into a streamy waterfall. And it looked artistic from the other side of the window, as bluish grey clouds covered the whole canvas with raindrops flowing downwards leaving its narrow path as watercolour. Besides being so alluring no one inside cared to appreciate it, well, why would they, when they are too busy making out.

Velvet blue walls and tiles from Cera with Italian dining and furniture, was the living room of Marina George, the fiancé of Richard Buthello. He was all over her on the sofa making out like animals. At least that's the case for one of them.

"Oh, Richi... What's up with you today?"

"Everything is... My life, my job, you, me and..." He kissed pulling her closer to every inch of his body. But the wildness went out off the couch when he hit the vase which was an imported Italian vase that her father had gifted.

"Shit... Richard, what have you done?"

"It's just a vase."

"My father brought it from Italy."

"Ok, it's just an Italian vase. Oh, come on like everything else here is Italian. Let's just ignore it."

He said getting upon her again. But she pushed him away and said.

"You are acting really weird today. You blasted on me for just scratching some piece of antique at your home, and now you just don't care about these kinda stuff. Something's up with you." She said getting ominous while he was baffled as to how to start with his recent charade.

"Yeah, it was a very important vase. You shouldn't have acted like this." He sounded more like he was apologizing than shouting while she gazed him as she knows he's guilty of something.

"Richard Buthello!" She exclaimed.

"Ok, fine. There's something I haven't told you. It's only because all that happened was somewhat weird and cannot be easily explained." And he started with the first chapter of his novel 'How not to give an interview'.

By the end of the story, it was clear by the looks of her frown face that she was deeply disappointed in him. But he was wondering why she wasn't showing any sympathy.

"How could you do this?" She literally was disappointed.

"How could I? What did I do? She did all this, Debora..." Before he could even finish the sentence she said.

"If you wanted my sympathy, then why didn't you tell me about it on the very first day of the interview. This is not a small matter to ignore. We are engaged now, and you were hiding it from me..."

It's funny how Richard actually thought she would give him a shoulder to cry on. Even after so many years of dating, he didn't learn that most women need to know everything about their man as soon as possible. The mood of romance ended, and Richard left her home.

A few days later, rain flooded the street around the facade of the company iHNS private limited. Richard jumped out of the cab right after paying him, to the paved streets and rushed towards CCD to protect his mobile and suitcase from the rain. Still, he got wet above his sleeves. As he entered the café, he saw Deborah D'mello sitting on the seat adjacent to him, busy on her phone and waiting for her coffee. She constantly kept glancing at the counter waiting and then her silver slim second-less dial watch.

"Does it take too long to get a coffee here?" Richard said meeting her.

"Apparently it's sooner than our cafeteria." She said offering the seat in front of her that was empty.

The waiter approached them bringing her a café latte, after which Richard gave him his order of an espresso.

"Well, it's been almost a week since we last, talked." He said and she questioned back. "Since HR office, you mean, right?" She asked and he smirked.

"I see," She said then gave a blow to her hot coffee and gave a kiss to the mug sipping it. Left a tint of red lips on the mug. The waiter brought his espresso, as Richard leaned forward to pick the mug she asked.

"What exactly do you think happened that day?"

"Mm... I don't know." He shrugged and she said. "You don't know? The way you were smiling that day, I almost figured out what kind of person you are."

"What do you mea... What kind of person do you think I am?"

"Narcissistic misogynist smug." She said staring her latte.

"That's rude and you are wrong on so many levels. Whatever you call me, but there's one thing I'm absolutely not, A misogynist." He said and she smirked.

"If I am then, it's only to one person." He smiled and continued, "And by the way, it felt really good that day when the HR bashed you." He said and she grinned.

"Mr Buthello, I might also add one more attribute... Childish."

"You judge too much," He sneered as he said, "And I'm not childish."

"Oh really? First, you complain to the principal of the school. Then expect me to get punished by her. Who thinks like that? It's a corporate world, Richard. You have worked for a corporate company before, haven't you?" She said and he felt humiliated.

"So, what happened that day?" He asked and she replied. "Do you know how long I have been working here?"

"Eh... No."

"For almost 7 years and nobody even talks to me without giving respect first. And that day, she asked me... requested me politely to assign both of you properly, nothing else." She then drank her latte and even Richard decided to respect the silence and finish his expresso at the same time. Not a single word uttered by both of them. As they stepped out of the Cafeteria, rain stormed their way. Deborah pulled out her blue umbrella out of the bag, opened it and looked at Richard for a second, who was standing on the edge of the shop, waiting for the rain to get over.

"You need a lift?" It was surprising that she asked him. He was confused, but he nodded and joined her under the blue umbrella. Their skin stuck together while walking still for the first time, being so close they didn't feel uncomfortable.

Later that day, at Deborah's home. Her pants being half wet, she removed it on the living room to avoid getting the floor wet. On pink panty and shirt buttoned out, she walked up to her bedroom.

"Shit! What the hell!" She screamed watching a young shirtless boy, 6', lying on her bed. He winked at her waving his hands over his crotch.

"Abhishek, I told you not to use that key without my permission." Deborah glared at him.

"Then why did you even give me an extra key?"

"I gave it because whenever I need you, I won't have to wear clothes to walk up to the living room and open the door. You understand that?" She said being firmer than his... Him.

"But, my college ended early and I needed you..." As he was saying she interrupted.

"You need me right now?" She walked closer to him unbuttoning her shirt.

"Yes, I do, indeed I do." He said, and she sat above his crotch removing her shirt. Kissed him on his hairs while he indulged into her boobs and their evening began...

Chapter 5

Knight and King

"The fuck does that mean?" Matthew Butthelo, Richard's younger brother, was shocked to know that, "Engagement is still on, she still and always will be the love of my life. It's just that we are taking somethings slow right now." Richard explained.

"You don't slow down the process after getting engaged; it's very wrong. You are literally on the verge of going from the break into break up."

"Don't you dare say that? This isn't even a break. These things happen in an adult relationship." Richard said.

"You won't even accept anything, maybe she was right calling you childish today." Matthew said, steering his car out of the highway.

"Matthew, I swear if you say one more word I'll tell our father about the condom and stash I found in this car's back seat. Then I'll see how you get this car."

"Sorry, I was just trying to help you. Just remember one thing, if you are hiding something from a girl, either make sure she never finds out about it or better would be, don't hide anything at all." Matthew said getting into the complex.

"Yeah, I don't need relationship advice from my younger brother."

"I am younger, but I have been in a relationship many times. So, I am more experienced than you."

"Having too many relations doesn't mean you are good at it, it certainly says you can't keep a relationship long enough. Long-term experience counts."

"Really? Well, I have most broke up experiences and trust me this is how it starts." He smirked parking it outside the C wing of the building. And after giving each other terrible advices they got home.

At the same time, Deborah's place. After the lovemaking, when he was getting dressed and she was getting ready for a shower, Abhishek said, "I have been waiting to ask you something."

"What?"

"Where are we at, now?" He asked and even after understanding the question she said, "My home."

"Phh... No! I am talking about our relationship. We are in a serious relationship, aren't we?" Abhishek was curious.

"You have a key to my apartment, I think that answers the question."

"Ok, but in a few months my college will get over and then... Eh... When will we get married?"

"Don't you think you are asking me too many questions?" She said, and Abhishek came close to her, holding her bare waist, he continued, "Hey, I'm serious. I love you and I wanna get married within a few years. You know before you age so that even you won't have any pro..." As he was speaking, she interrupted loosening his hands off her waist.

"Wait a minute. What do you mean before I age?"

"Huh?" Abhishek was baffled.

"You think I am getting old." She gave him a dirty look.

"No! You are hot as hell," He tried to make it up, "Seriously hot for a 27-year-old lady." But screwed up even more.

"Abhishek! I am exhausted right now so don't spoil my mood even more. Better leave ASAP... we will talk later." She said and he nodded innocently and left. The moment he closed the door, she had a sigh of relief. "Oh! Serious relation-shit!" And walked towards the bathroom.

Next day weekend started. Right one week after their Non-Break period, Richard went to surprise Marina at her apartment. The rain decided to take a leave that noon, so he went all neat on his bike. Taking a deep breath, he rang the bell. Marina, chuckling on her way opened the door. Her smile tipped off as she saw Richard standing baffled.

"Hi, I wanted to surprise you." He wasn't that excited about seeing her so much happy, "Is someone with you right now?"

"Yes, and for your own good, I really wish you would have called before coming here." She shrugged with a mixed expression of confusion and poker face. And that expression triggered Richard's overthinking sensation.

"Well, I jus... Since we are engaged, I can come anytime." He said, forcing a smile as he walked straight inside curiously to the living room and found out, not who but with whom she was spending time with.

"Hi, Richard..." Said both the girls with grumpy ass face.

"Ha... Hi." He said and whispered to Marina, "I really should have called." And she giggled.

After Marina's college got over, she hadn't been in contact with many friends. Except for two of her best friends, Deeksha and Karishma. And they two are the person Richard hates the most. Back then when he first proposed Marina, those two tried to break something which didn't even start. Finally, when Richard asked, "Now I'm not asking you to settle anything with me, I only want an answer, it will only be for me. Just forget about everything anyone says or think about me and tell me only what YOU think, do you love me?" Though the way Richard said was a lot confusing to understand but she did catch the feeling of what he meant. And the result of that proposal is so clear now, well they are engaged so obviously she said yes. And from then not her friends nor Richard liked each other.

"She told us everything." Deeksha said.

"Yes, and we are not even surprised anymore. It was expected." Karishma added.

"Hey, I said I was really sorry, and I promised that I won't hide anything ever again..."

"Ok, so I suppose, you came here to make up for what you did, right?" Deeksha asked.

"Yes and..."

"But you didn't bring anything for making up to her, even a rose would have done a better job."

Deeksha was literally overacting. But this didn't affect Marina's mind at all. She just chuckled all the way along. Eventually, when they were getting too hard on him, she came in between smiling and said.

"Deeksha, Karishma, stop and Richard you don't have to say anything anymore." Then she raised her left hand, showing him the ring and continued, "It's still on and always will be. It was just a small fight; you don't have to worry about anything."

"I love you." His voice matched the feeling of his eyes.

"I love you too." She said holding her arms around his neck.

"Deeksha, Karishma bubye." Marina said and they left.

"I missed you, more than anything." He said.

"I missed you too... Shall we catch up from where we left off last time?" She asked and he lifted her from the couch to the bedroom. Everything went back to normal. Later that night both their family went on a joint dinner at Fortune select Exotica Hotel.

Monday, back to iHNS, as Richard was done with his work he went up, to have a word with Deborah. He knocked on the door and she said, "Come in."

She wore a black pencil skirt and a peach coloured top. He went in formals, cream shirt and grey pant, for an informal meet. Trying to be friendly, he sat on the chair smiling. They were having a casual conversion about his new post and nothing personal. Then all of a sudden Richard glanced over a King piece of chess. Which was larger than a regular chess piece.

"Is that just a showpiece or there's a hidden chess board lying here somewhere?" Richard asked mockingly.

"That's not a showpiece nor a real piece; it's my award." A tint of pride on her face shined.

"Award? You are an award-winning chess player?" He asked with a look of surprise on his face.

"Yes, what makes it so much surprising?"

"Just never heard of a woman winning awards in chess."

"So, I was right. A misogynist." Deborah said raising her left eyebrow.

"I was talking in general." He said, and she instantly put out a chess game on her tablet and challenged Richard for a match. "Can you pla... Do you know how to play chess?"

"Of course, I do" He pulled his chair closer to the desk and gazing her, he said, "Shall we?"

Deborah lets him play as white, ergo he played the first move. He moved the pawn of his right side standing ahead of the knight. Then she moved her pawn that was ahead of her knight. By Richard's first move itself, she understood that he was an amateur player. On the other hand, he couldn't figure out Deborah's any move henceforth. Richard was nothing professional, but he did know how to apply the rules properly. Regardless of the situation in Richard's hand, he was no match for her. She is a professional state level chess player; she might have practically studied all of the rules quite well.

A few moments later, when the game got interesting, all her colleagues started to join the game one by one in her cabin, which made it difficult for Richard to concentrate. By that time, she had lost a few pawns and a knight while he was short of both the knights, bishops and a rook. This had him wondering that she had a few chances before to checkmate him but didn't. He later realized how this could be more humiliating with losing all his players dying than just a normal checkmate. And he actually was humiliated. At last, like slitting his throat with a knife after torture she checkmated him by one of her knights.

"Good game." He faked a smile, but she didn't have to fake as she said, "Of course!"

Chapter 6

Smokey lies

A shes of the burned flake fell down along the drops of rain, falling above her, as Deborah flicks her cigarette.

Drops of rain fell as bullet shots as Richard cuts through the stormy rain. He slowed down as his company approached, saw Deborah under her blue umbrella, smoking as always.

Her eyes looked cunning, constipated stare when she smiled at him. He smiled back, smirked as he parked his bike right in front of her. She blew a smoke at him while he removed the key from his bike. He didn't react at all and walked straight to the company. She giggled when he left. Later in their workplace when he was on his way to meet TL Shree, passing by the cabin of miss D'mello. He kept glaring her through the blurred glass window. He never missed the sight whenever he passed that area. His eyes filled with hate, glancing with rage and thoughts of bringing her down of what she thinks of as her throne.

After an hour at the cafeteria, buying his meal Richard walked in search of a seat. He saw Idhaya having lunch alone, so he joined her.

"Hi Richard, after a long time."

"Yes, after a long pathetic time." He chuckled.

"So how are you, "ENJOYING" here?" She asked quoting.

"It's fine working here, what about you? Hope you are working as financial... Whatever that is you do." Richard asked.

"Yeah, everything is just fine here too. And tell me, what else is happening?" She asked pushing her question.

"Nothing... Much." He was sceptical of what to say.

Then the conversation stopped as his eyes shifted towards a girl, who was walking straight to him. She smiled on the way and as a courtesy, he smiled back. Then she kept her lunch on the table and said, "Hi Idhaya." And laughed while Richard hid his face with his palm in embarrassment.

"What did I miss right now?" Idhaya asked.

"Not a thing, seriously!" Richard exclaimed mockingly.

"Anyway, hi. I am Sheetal." She said.

"Hello, I'm Richard."

"Oh! You are Richard. Heard so much about you." She was surprised to meet him.

"What've you heard about?" Richard asked.

"Just about our first meet and little with Deborah." Idhaya added.

"Oh, yeah that... Ok." Richard then starts eating as Sheetal and Idhaya got back to their previous gossip. Idhaya was telling

Sheetal about the time when her fiancé came to surprise her in Pune after their 6-month anniversary.

"That was the best day of my life, I was so much frustrated that day, but after seeing Johan right in front of my eyes, made my day. It was the best feeling ever. He and his friend came all the way from Kalyan to Pune on his scooter just to surprise me. We weren't even engaged at that time." After she was done with her story and Richard was almost finished with his meal. He said, "My story is not that interesting, nothing long distance or anything. But just a long-term relationship goes back to my college life." Hearing that both Idhaya and Sheetal were baffled.

"About whom, are you talking?" Idhaya asked.

"Oh, I haven't told you about her. Marina George, I'm also engaged." He smiled.

"Seriously! You are in a serious relationship, then too you just randomly hit on anyone." Sheetal was shocked and so was Idhaya.

"Hey, I wasn't hitting on you. I smiled back just as a courtesy."

"Alright, so what about Deborah."

"What? No! No way in hell. Who would even give you that thought?" Richard asked, and she turned her head towards Idhaya. She sneered shrugging, "Don't blame it on me, I only told her what I've heard."

"What have you heard? And from whom?" He was curiously shocked.

"The whole office is talking about you, that in your free time you play chess in her office. All the time lurking around her cabin, staring... Is it true?" Idhaya asked, and he went speechless for a moment.

"Wha... no... eh... No! This is ridiculous." He exclaimed.

"I thought of that, but then someone saw you both in CCD outside last week, walking down the road under the same umbrella. It sounded so romantic, so I guessed it might be true." She said cheerfully but Richard burst out on her angrily.

"It's not true, I FUCKING hate her!" He was changed, high-pitched, "She's an egoistic mind sucking bitch."

"Richard, calm down. Anyway... eh, my lunch time is over and we better leave now. Take it easy... buddy, bubye." They had to keep a distance from erupting Richard before he goes too vile.

Later he noticed that most of the staff there was staring Richard, waiting for him to interact with Deborah. All they wanted was some drama in the office, that was making him a little insecure.

At the end of the day, Richard was getting outside of the company. Deborah was standing aside the entrance. Holding a cigarette as always but it was yet to be lit.

"Heard you were lurking around my office all day."

"Most people hear what they want to hear." Richard smirked.

"You must really be on a special level of illusion that I would want you even around me." Deborah's pride was as high as her chin.

And by Richard's face, it was obvious that he was done with all the bullshit she put up with him.

"That's it; I am just gonna cut to the chase and say it, I despise you... I hate you..." Said staring at her while standing uncomfortably close to her.

"Oh! I am shocked." She said quickly like she didn't care. Then she lit the cigarette and after taking a puff she asked.

"Richard, you're a creep. Have you never seen a lady smoke before?"

"Seen a lot, but not as much as you do."

"It's enough to kill me, happy?" Even her question felt like it was dominating him.

"Satisfied." No more words by Richard.

"Are you going to smoke with me?"

"I don't smoke." Richard said and she replied, "Then stop blocking me." Blowing a smoke towards his face while he mumbles as he walks away, audible enough for her to listen. "Alright bitch."

Later, when he reached home, he removed his raincoat and threw it away. Walked straight towards the balcony. As he opened the door, he saw his younger brother, Mathew, smoking a cigarette. Mathew stopped puffing as he entered. There was a moment of silence. Then Richard raised his palm like he was ordering Mathew to hand over the cigarette. He handed, Richard looked at it, flicking it, he took a puff.

"You look stressed bro, is everything ok?" Mathew asked.

"Just fine..." Richard replied.

"You know, the other day I met Marina at the mall. We talked a little and then she asked me. 'You are looking out for Richard, Right?'"

"Then what did you say?" Richard asked.

"Well, I said, you don't have to worry about him. He hasn't touched a single cigarette in a very long time." Mathew said and Richard stared at him in bewilderment for a moment. Then they both burst out laughing as that was the joke of the day. Mathew kept chuckling as he said.

"I was thinking, man! We smoke every day together, the hell did I just tell her."

"Bro she should never find out about this. Well, after all, that is happening, it's better she knows a little less now." Richard said calming his laugh.

"Well, how did she react about the chess game with Deborah?" Mathew asked.

"I obviously didn't tell her about that."

"Eh... But you were supposed to tell her everything about these stuffs, right?" Mathew was being moral.

"Come on, it's pointless to share everything. And it was just a game, nothing much to fuss about."

"Alright, alright." Mathew said and after taking a puff he asked, "You... are serious with Marina, right?"

"Matt! Don't ever ask me that question again. I love her."

Chapter 7

Eyes that threatens

A room full of school and college students sitting one on one in opposite chairs and among all those children sat Richard. He looked very much like a professor but was, in fact, a student there. The person sitting next to Richard was a 52-year-old man, a chess master. And there at Chess Academy, Richard went back to school learning chess.

"I still don't understand, why do you want to learn chess now. At this age?" The master said in low pitch.

"I have been always interested in chess since childhood. But never got a chance to learn before, so I'm learning now." Richard said, cutting the black bishop with his white knight.

"That's a lie." Master caught him in no time.

"That's not, how could you just think that?" He giggled as he asked.

"If you were so much keen on chess then you wouldn't be playing like shit... Check!"

"Fine, it's just that, being a team leader, I should know my employee. And chess improves in reading the mind so that's why I am..." Master didn't even let him finish the sentence as he said, "It's believable but not true."

"Well, why are you so much interested in knowing my reason? You got a student, so I guess that's a good thing for you." Richard was a little arrogant.

"Hmm... In chess, it is very important to know the opponent's character, nature and mind. It helps in predicting their next move and make our chances to win greater."

"So, is that why you are defeating me so easily right now?" Richard asked while he was confused as to which move he should do next.

"Oh no, I don't have to use any tricks on you. The way you play chess, I could even defeat you blindfolded." He mocked Richard, but he kept his anger under the skin. Because no matter how much humiliation he gets, it would be nothing like what he got in that chess game he played with Deborah. Needless to say, he went home after getting checkmated by the master.

One fine day, when Richard was halfway towards his office, he saw Deborah waiting by her car, stressed. Her car had a flat tire and because of heavy rain, public transport was in scarce. As Richard was on his bike, he saw her standing there helpless. At first, he just ignored her but then, don't know what made him come back to her. As he slowed his bike, she got anxious about what he was going to say. No doubt she was ready to give him a comeback.

"Hi, you seemed troubled." He said.

"Tire is punctured and I am late for my meeting, nothing much." She ended with a fake smile.

"If you want, I can drop you." He said formally.

"And why would you do that?" She asked.

"Alright." He took a sigh of relief to say this. "Ever since after the HR meeting, I have been trying to improve our relation. As a colleague and co-worker, I always thought to have a mutual understanding in a workplace. But you always tried to piss me off. Now again, I am directly trying to maintain the mutual understanding..."

"Alright... thank you." She said and they waited for a little until the tow truck took away her car. She then sat on the seat of his bike and opened her umbrella.

"Have you ever ridden on a bike before, in the monsoon?" Richard asked while starting his bike.

"No... Usually, I don't, Why?" She asked.

"No reason... Just hold on to your umbrella." He said and gradually started the ride.

Richard was completely covered in a raincoat while Deborah, wearing cream pants and olive-green shirt, only had her blue umbrella. Then the cloudburst with a heavy storm and at that moment Richard sped his bike. With one hand, she had held him tightly by his waist while another left loose on the umbrella. Her umbrella flew far away from his bike and she kept screaming.

"Richard, stop! Richard fucking stop." She screamed in his ears continuously tapping his shoulder with the other hand. "Wha... what happened?" Richard asked chuckling.

"Just stop it. I want my umbrella back." She said and he replied, "Ok, go get it." He said quite calmly.

She was breathing angrily, but getting completely wet under the rain made her look like a cute angry puppy, which Richard felt was really funny. And his expression was like a pressure cooker about to blow a whistle of laughs. She walked across the street where the wind took her umbrella and after bringing it back she said, "You can go now, I don't need your assistance anymore."

"Hey, this was rain. Don't blame this on me. By the way, water is logged ahead and I don't think you would be able to walk over that without getting your pants wet." His concern didn't appear so real on his face, yet he tried to be a little more supportive.

"I am already wet, so it doesn't matter." She gazes through his eyes.

"Fine, I am not waiting anymore. Bye. But yeah, that water is coming from the near sewage and not to forget the dumpster around it. All the best." He said and started his ride.

"Wait!" She said and sat on his bike, "I swear I will make your life hell out here if you fuck shit up now."

"Firstly, that wasn't my fault before and I will try to slow down now." Richard said and again gradually rode the bike. The moment he entered the waterlogged area, because of potholes his bike was slowing down. So, he said to her, "Deborah D'mello, good luck" and he rapidly speeds up splashing all the water on the back wetting her pants with mudding water. The moment they reached the company. She instantly jumped off the bike. Giving him a dirty look she said.

"Richard Buthello, Thank-you so much for your help. I will surely payback with the same as soon as I get a chance." She said in a subtle way while her voice was pleasant but her eyes spoke of rage. Richard just nodded controlling his uncontrollable laugh, but as she was on her way to the entrance. She turned with her half-ass facing Richard and said "Good luck!" And at that instant, all his uncontrollable laughs went off to unsettling silence.

Chapter 8

The fun began

Deborah D'mello held it in her hand as Abhishek looked at her with love. She had a firm grip on it with both of her hands, and she puts in her mouth, biting it as it gets inside. He kept smiling all the way until she made a sour face, removing it out of her mouth. Getting embarrassed Abhishek asked, "Is it too salty?"

"Yes, and also it's too big." Deborah said.

"No problem. I'll cut it in pieces if you want." He said and also wiped the white that was left on her lips with his hands and licked it. Then he took a knife and cut the sandwich into four pieces, then added more mayonnaise on it.

"Why are you making a sandwich all of a sudden?" She asked.

"You know, I read it on the internet that the way to a woman's heart is through her stomach." Abhishek said.

"It might be true but for that, the food should be really good." She replied and his face paled down.

"It's alright. I like your efforts. Want a blowjob." She asked and gave him a good time. Later that day at the office, Deborah was with one of her employees discussing the budget plans and at that moment entered Richard in the office. She was staring at him as he walked between the cabins. Her employee asked, "Wow, Nice choice Debora..." As she was speaking Deborah interrupted.

"Shh... Mind your own damn business." She said with her arrogance while eyes stuck at Richard. As he was just looking around, he sighted Deborah, who was deadpan staring at him. They both shared the glares as he passed, then at the end she smiled. Her smile was not an ordinary one but had hidden devious game behind it. And the fact that Richard understands her smile freaked the shit out of him. He walked deadpan down the row.

Of course, she was not going to just become friends with someone who had recently painted her meeting attire half muddy brown. So, she went to meet Team leader Shree. Shree is a superior TL of Richard and other TLs.

"Miss Deborah! I Didn't expect to see you here." Shree exclaimed as she just walked in through the doors.

"Well, on the contrary, I never had to come here before." She said and stood opposite his desk.

"Have a seat." He offered.

"No need. I won't be here that long." She said getting straight to her point, "I'm here to discuss a few... Situations," and continued. "Just so you know, I am one of the few people who knows about your partner." She said and he replied casually "My partner? I'm married to her. Everyone knows abou..."

"I am not talking about your wife, but the one with whom you have been slutting around from the past few months."

"I... Eh... I don't understand a word you are saying. You are accusing me of something... Mm... I never did." He stammered.

"Well, I don't care whether you accept or not. I somehow got your wife's number too. Let's see what she says." Deborah said.

"Deborah, are you trying to blackmail me? What do you even want from me? wait!" He stopped worrying, "So, you have my wife's number and you know a few things that my friends know too, but what makes you think she is going to believe you. And none of my friends even like you, nobody does. So, you won't even get any witnesses to prove that I have slept with Heer. So, I don't care what you want from me, but I won't help you." He leaned back in his chair getting comfortable. At that moment, she felt helpless and silently started walking out.

"Deborah! I have one proposition for you. I have always found you cute and hot too. So, I might help you if you help me out after the work." Shree said checking her out. She smiled as she replied "Richard is doomed and you are going to help me wreck his life." and left the cabin.

A few moments later Shree received a voice message from Deborah. "... And none of my friends like you, nobody does. So, you won't even get any witness to prove that I have slept with Heer. So, I don't care what you want from me, but I won't help you..." Apparently the whole time Deborah was in the room, she recorded their conversation on her mobile phone. She texted "Thanks for your words. Also, what you said at the end to me was the cherry on top of the cake. I am just one 'SEND' away from ruining your marriage if you don't do my simple work."

Well, what's left for Shree to say. Reluctantly he had to fuck up Richard's life at the office and he started it in the evening.

"Richard, May I have a word with you?" Shree asked stepping into his office

"Yes, sir." Richard replied, getting ready to leave.

"See, I have to tell you this. It's been more than a month now since you are working here and you are doing good..."

"Doing good... Is there a but?" Richard asked.

"Yes, But it's not good enough." Shree said and Richard's face turned pale.

"Since it was the start of your work, I was lenient on you, but the company won't run any better if this is your pace." He said joining hands below the waist as he faced away.

"But sir, I am trying my best here."

"Your best isn't the best for the company. So, let's start today. I am afraid you have to do overtime till 8 pm. Finish it all and we will set you with the new program tomorrow."

"But Shree listen, you don't understand..." Richard said and Shree stopped and glared at him.

"Apology, I mean Sir, my family planned a dinner with my fiancé's family. They didn't know that I have been given over time, they are already at the hotel." Richard said while Shree went speechless with guilt. Then with a firm voice, he said "I can't help you even if I want to. It's not up to me. My hands are tied and the orders are from above. Good luck." He said and left Richard in distress.

"Nice. I am completely satisfied with your help. In fact, it gave me more pleasure than expected. You even said good luck. Great job!" Deborah texted back to the audio of the conversation recorded by Shree himself. Well, Deborah needed a confirmation as it is obvious, she doesn't trust anyone.

Chapter 9

Good luck

Brown leather Derby's shoe, Cambridge cotton black pant with its brown leather belt, cream shirt tinted green from Oxford and citizen's gold 24-carat watch was the attire of Richard Buthello at the office. After dealing with the candidates he was on his way to his cabin to check his reports. The moment he entered his office-space he was shocked to see who was inside. Blue shirt from Zara, her favourite. White Pencil skirt and black heels. Sat Deborah D'mello at his chair inside his cabin.

"Why do I always find a what-have-I-seen look in your face whenever you see me, terrified?" She was mocking him.

"What are you doing here?" He walked closer to the desk and added, "And that chair belongs to me."

"You aren't that shameless to ask a lady out of her seat," She ended with a low pitch. "Are you?"

"Of course, not." He said and sat on the front chair.

"I was just walking down here, so I thought, I will just give a visit to a friend." She said raising her left eyebrow.

"So, after our conversation are you going to visit that friend?" He was being rhetorically sarcastic.

"Well..." Coming to the point she said "Just tell me one thing, Richard. How do you like working here? Enjoying?"

"A lot. So much that yesterday I just skip my family dinner with my fiancé just so I could enjoy my overtime." He cherished dramatically.

"Fiancé? You failed to mention that before. How is she? Does she love you?" She was trying hard to hurt him subtly.

"We are engaged. I guess that answers your question?"

"Only if engagement is a post. So, what happens when you get promoted to marriage? Do love changes or remains the same? Would she change or leave you? Because a lot of change happens in behaviour when people get promoted."

"I don't know why I am even discussing this with you. Whether she changes or not, she will always love me and I will too. But you and your corporate mind won't understand. As some people aren't capable of feeling love." He smirked being an asshole to her.

"I hate... to agree on anything with you. Perhaps you are right on this. Love is not meant for me. Love is tragic. It drives mind to go insane. Especially when the marriage breaks, cheating on partners or so many other things to account. But I just wish that you don't face any of those problems."

Oh yes, she wishes it and even he knows she does. Then while leaving the cabin she turned to him, standing at the door and said, "Give my regards to your fiancé and... GOOD LUCK, with your future." She said and he smiled. Then when she left he noticed something unusual and kept thinking about it.

Chapter 10
Screenshot

She blinked her glistening eyes looking in the mirror after she was done eye lining. Then had a kiss of the red lips stick. Turns around and before leaving the mirror, she looked back. Back to her ass, checking how thick it looks with the jeans. Deborah smiled and walked towards the window. Sliding the curtains, she exclaimed "Oh! Fuck no." As she sighted rain from 18th floor shuttering into the city.

Coming down the elevator, she bashed her car mechanic through a phone call. "Listen to me carefully. Firstly, I am getting late. Secondly, it's raining like shit outside and thirdly my car was supposed to be ready three days ago. What's your answer now?"

"Madam, my answer will remain same as before. These problems take time to get repaired. Just give me one day and your car will be as good as new."

Grinning as she speaks, "If I don't get my car soon enough, I will see how your company would work again."

She reached the gates of her building and opened her blue umbrella. Walked towards the rickshaw stand struggling herself from not getting her jeans wet. She was clearly not fond of rain.

After an hour she reached her office. She was half an hour late. Since traffic was everywhere because of the rain, they were allowed to come late that morning. Even Richard came late to the office. And eventually, everything was set back to normal in there. But then, something happened, the rain worsened and the situation changed completely. By noon trains stopped working and as a result traffic spiked. In a few hours, the water level rose and the city got under flood.

Richard received a call from Shree. He told him to leave the office as soon as possible. He told his candidates and also reached out to Idhaya to go home. And in a few minutes, the word was out that the city was under flood. It was a complete mayhem in the office as everyone was trying to rush out of the building at once. Richard felt the same crowd as a local train when he was coming out of the building. Finally, he had a sigh of relief when he stepped out of the building. But his view was blurry as rain stood strong as glass in front. He never saw it fall this strong and thick before in his entire life. He got scared and nervous, but anyhow he needed to get home so he took his bike and started riding.

Traffic was like a group of ants stuck in a narrow barrel. If it wasn't for the bike, Richard couldn't even cross a kilometre of the journey. Most of the cars and other big vehicles, even rickshaw couldn't move an inch. Only the biker got the upper hand but that too not for much long. As he waited for half an hour in the same place like a statue, the water level reached his knees even after being on a bike.

He received a call from Shree. Carefully saving his phone from the rain, he picked the call. "Richard, where are you now?" Shree asked.

"I am just stuck in traffic for almo..."

"Are you anywhere near the office?"

"Yes, quite near."

"Great! Come back. There's no way the traffic is going to get clear. And from what I have heard, the flood is going to increase within a few hours."

"But I can't come back. You don't understand the situation here. I can't even move my bike to the corner."

"Richard, ditch the bike and come back. I have been calling back every employee and it's not just me. Every department in this building, in fact, every corporate company is a home today. It's a matter of your life and also an order from me. Come back to the office." The intensity in his voice described the gravity of the situation in a matter of seconds.

"Eh... Yes. Yes, sir, I am coming." He said and somehow, he managed to take his bike around the corner and parked it out there. Well, it was sinking half under the water but he realized his life was more important so he left it. He was brisk walking with water reaching his thighs. As he crossed a few meters of his walk, he spotted her. Sitting in a cab with an attitude on her face.

"Hey, Deborah." He knocked on her window.

She was surprised to see him out there. But she didn't even lower down her window and asked. "What are you doing out here?" Because of the rain, he couldn't understand a word she said so he signalled her to lower down the window. But she just shook her head saying. "No no no..."

Richard made a poker face and eventually, she lowered it. "Yes, what do you want?" She asked.

"What do I want? Deborah! Don't you know what's happening out here?" He said hyperventilating. "Of course, I do. That's why I left early today. Still, I am stuck here with this dumb cab driver." She replied.

Hearing that Richard went speechless for a moment. Like how could someone be so mean and selfish? He said, "So that's how you reached this far in a cab. Because you knew about the situation and left early. Anyway, now what's your plan?"

"What plan? I am in a cab, going home what else." She said ruthlessly while her driver hit his head with his palm. "Never mind. Carry on... Happy journey." Richard said nodding his head slowly and was about to leave. Then he realized he wasn't as mean as her and just because of a little humanity, he had, he went back to her and said. "Deborah, what you are doing is the dumbest idea of all. And this traffic is going to stick here forever. Just for your own sake came back to the office. All of us are going back and will stay there itself until the flood is gone. Now it's all up to you." He said and even her frustrated driver also supported him so that she could get out of the cab.

"Eww... fuck!" Was the first word came out of her mouth when she stepped out. Walking through the muddy water that was almost above her knees. It was no doubt the grossest thing she had ever done. She was more worried about getting dirty than that of dying in floods. Richard was leading the way while Deborah was following his lead. He never thought he would actually help her in his life and neither did she. Then a patch came where water was reaching almost her waist as she was a little short. She was scared to death to cross that patch while the office, iHNS was just one block away. She was hesitating to move a muscle forward and Richard was done with her leisure act. He pulled her into the water holding her hand and forcefully crossed the waterlogged area. He held her palm firm till the end. They ran so fast that a few times water went into her mouth.

Hyperventilating as she said, "Richard Buthello! How dare you touch me?"

"I was only trying to help you!" He exclaimed.

"Who said I needed your help? And because of you... Ew, that dirty water is inside my mouth."

"Oh really! Be happy at least you are not drowning under it." He said angrily and walked into the building. And she just stood there with her mixed thoughts.

A few minutes later in the office. Everyone came back safely while the city remained unsafe. They had enough food for everyone because of the canteen. The situation was handled properly. They all were out of their cabins, together all staffs and TLs talking about stuff. Except for Deborah. She sat alone inside her cabin overthinking everything that happened to her that day.

Then she received a call; it was of Abhishek. "Baby! Are you ok? Heard about the flood in the city. You are fine ri..." As he was speaking she interrupted.

"I told you not to call me when I am in the office. Why did you call then?"

"Deborah, I was worried about you."

"What worried? I am fine, you don't have to worry about me."

"Ok, I am sorry and if you want to know then I am also fine... Eh safe."

"Good, bye." She said hanging up the phone and instantly opened WhatsApp and wrote a message.

Within 10 minutes when Richard checked the notification, he saw that it was a message from Deborah. Reading the message, he felt like laughing, but it also made him happy. He responded back nicely to the text and later texted his brother Matthew.

"You won't believe, who texted me today. Well, you won't even believe what happened today."

"Sorry, forgot to ask you. Are you safe? Also, tell me what happened." Matthew replied.

"I am safe back in office. Mostly we all are spending the night here. And I am sending you the screenshot of the text." He said and went to Deborah's chat box. After taking a screenshot, he opened the picture. Clicked on share via WhatsApp. Searched Matthew in M and sent him the screenshot. A few seconds later he received a reply from Matthew. "Bro when are you sending the screenshot?" Richard was baffled to know he didn't send her the screenshot. But he was sure he did send it. When he checked properly, he was even more baffled to find out that instead of Matthew in M names section he sent the screenshot to Marina, his fiancé. The only words came out of his mouth were, "Oh, Fuck no!"

Chapter 11

End of the day

Richard was panicking, going to and fro inside his cabin. Mumbling to himself "What the fuck! What the fuck! What the fuck!" Then he called his brother. Matthew picked up the call but he was silent. "Matthew! Are you there? Matthew! Matthew!"

"Mmm... Yes, yes, I am here. What's up? Are you alright?"

"No! I mean, yes. I am safe from the flood, but I fucked up." Richard said.

"What did you do?"

"Just now when I was about to send you a screenshot of my conversation with Deborah."

"With Deborah? Ok."

"Yes, well, I by mistakenly sent it to Marina and it's delivered... It's on read... fucking blue tick!" He exclaimed.

"Marina! Bro, how could you be so stupid. And what was the conversation about?"

"Dude, both your names start with M. I didn't notice and clicked her name instead of you." Richard said.

"But what was the conversation?" Mathew asked and he said.

"Ok, ok listen, "Hi Richard this is Deborah. I just want to tell you that I am sorry. And I mean it and It's not only for today but for everything I have done in the past month. I know I was a bitch to you, but you weren't so good to me either. And I am even sick of all the child play we do to each other. To be honest, I am still scared and if it wasn't for you, I would have been dead. You saved my life today and I am grateful for that. Also, I am looking forward to our friendship" This is what she said to me."

Richard said after reading out the message to him and he replied, "It's ok. Not a big deal. There's nothing to worry about, brother."

"Yes, yes, there is because after that I replied to her that I am also looking forward to our friendship. And no matter how much I have hated you, I did also have a soft point for you and that's why I was willing to do anything to save you today." After Richard had said this, their conversation went on a road to silence for a moment.

"Matt? Are you still there?" His voice begged for a sound.

"Yes, I am just trying to figure out what you just said."

"Bro, I was just trying to be polite like a gentleman. I know it sounds way different than wha..."

"Wait, Richard... Just wait, I have a plan."

"What? Is it a good plan?" Richard was very anxious.

"Maybe it is but it's our only way out."

"Fine, tell me." Richard said and they had a brief discussion. Then after the phone call, he checked his WhatsApp and yes, he did receive a reply from Marina.

"????" That's all she replied. He was wondering why she didn't say anything but anyway, he was prepared to reply now. So, he wrote.

"Honey, as you know about the floods. I helped her cross a few roads. But she was too scared and that is why she was exaggerating it a bit too much. Anyway, just because she is senior here. I thought this could be a good opportunity to improve our friendship. So there won't be any trouble in my work. And I didn't want any secrets between so I sent you the screenshot directly. Love you." He sent it and waited for fifteen minutes for her reply.

But his message wasn't even marked blue tick so to avoid any more frustration, he kept his phone in silent mode in his pocket and went out of his cabin. It was getting dark outside. A few were talking on the phone, few were chatting with each other and few were resting. But the rain wasn't taking a break. He saw Deborah through her blurred glass door. Inside and isolated from everyone. As he was about to walk up there, he stumbled into Idhaya.

"Oh! So sorry." Richard said.

"It's ok Richi..." As casually as she had always been.

"Glad you are still here, it's a mess outside." Richard said.

"I didn't leave the office in the first place. You all went running and came back running again while I was here watching your show." She said chuckling.

"Yeah, great. You enjoyed our suffering. It was funny for you, not for us."

"Come on, I am just kidding." Idhaya said.

"But why didn't you leave? I told you to leave." Richard asked and she replied.

"Actually, Johan was going to pick me up from my office. But he had to stay back in the studio. Mumbai got more floods than Navi Mumbai and he is there."

"I forgot, what is he doing? As in a job?" Richard asked.

"Johan is a journalist."

"Journalist! So they aren't sending him to cover the floods?"

"Oh no! He used to be in these types of crime and tragedy show before but not anymore. Now he does celebrity interviews of junior artists and small people. It's not that famous show yet, but he is happy, so doesn't matter." Idhaya replied. And then Idhaya joined her friends Sheetal and Daniya. Then, before knocking the doors of Deborah, he checked his phone and yes, he received a reply from Marina. It said,

"Richard, I want you to know I trust you. Yes, I was worried before but not anymore. I know you would never cheat on me, you don't even have to prove anything to me anymore. But thanks for showing your trust by sending the screenshot. Take care now; bye, love you too." Reading that message he smiled and walked back into his office.

The next day everything went back to normal from rain to local train. And everybody had a sigh of relief after watching the sun.

"I missed you, buddy." Richard said with a smile as the rays fall on his face. He then went to find his bike which was lying more than a kilometre away. His bike was in no condition to be working, so he dragged it to the nearest mechanic shop and gave it for repair. Then he took a cab and went home. At noon when Deborah reached home, she got angry to see Abhishek sitting inside without even consenting her.

"What are you doing inside my apartment?"

"Baby I was worried. How are you? Are you alright, nothing happened to you, right?" He said trying to hug her but he was stopped.

"I told you I was fine. And stop worrying about me like I am a child. I am anyway older than you." Her voice sounded annoyed.

"Deb... Why are you talking like this? I am your boyfriend. I am supposed to be worried about you."

"No, you don't need to be worried. Now stop irritating me, I am already stressed out and need to rest, so leave."

"Deborah, this is too much."

"What is?"

"I love you." Abhishek said, but she didn't utter a word.

"I knew it. All I hoped was for you to love me back just like I do. But you don't even give a shit about me. You were just using me all this time like a sex toy."

"Abhishek, you are my boyfriend. Now don't create a big scene out here. Today is not the day, please." She begged facing away.

"No! Just say I love you too. Is that so hard?"

"I am too restless to say anything right now. We will talk about this later."

"No, we won't. I can't do this anymore. I have feelings. I am not some cold-blooded, heartless bi... huh... this is over." He said with tears rolling out while she stood boldly, "It's over? Fine! I only care about myself. And I won't let anyone hurt me. So, go ahead. Drop the keys and just leave!" And he left throwing the keys on the floor, covering his face to stop crying while she slams the door and walks inside distressed.

A week later, at the end of the day in her office. While Richard was out there with his friends Deborah stood alone waiting for her cab.

Richard was with Idhaya and her friends Sheetal and Daniya. Then out of nowhere came Johan on his bike to surprise Idhaya. He came in his customized cruiser bike and looked handsome as Idhaya always mentioned. Idhaya introduced Johan to Richard and others.

"She talks a lot about you. Trust me, it feels like we have practically met you already." Richard said and Idhaya blushed. And as they were talking, even Marina came to surprise Richard. He just ran into her. Got in her car and kissed her while Idhaya sat on Johan's bike. And among all these people, one was there watching it all.

Deborah, standing aloof from any companion and compassion. She felt like a part of her was missing at that moment. For the first time, she was sad as she realized how lonely her life was. And it wasn't because of the recent breakup she had as it was clear that she never loved him before. But she was depressed because she couldn't love anyone anymore. She stood there with the sunset just waiting for something she doesn't even know about.

Chapter 12

What the Puff

Dew-kissed rose shimmered as the rays from rising sun passed through it into the room of Marina George. As she rests her head on Richard's bare chest while wearing his shirt. He woke up first when the rays fall on his eyelid. Then he raised his hand towards the sun, hiding the rays from falling upon Marina's eyes. He didn't want her to be disturbed in her sleep, but his little movement woke her up anyway. She looked up to him with a smile. A smile that said I am lucky to have you. He pulled her up by her shoulder, she wore nothing but just his shirt. Then, as she kissed him on his lip, he grabbed her ass like soft silky pillows. And thus, in the morning their night started again.

An hour later, Richard was getting ready. He wore his pants, shoes and also the Citizen watch. But not the shirt.

"I have to go now, please give me my shirt." Richard blushed.

"No, you won't get it. Stay or go shirtless your choice." Marina smiled.

"I will come back soon honey. I can't miss my class today."

"It's Sunday. You don't have to go anywhere today. And it's just a stupid chess class. I can teach you that. What do you say?

Want to play chess?" She said opening a few buttons of the shirt and he chuckled.

"Don't do that. I am tired now." Then he came closer and held by her shoulder, and he started kissing her on the neck. As he moved his kiss from neck to her lips, he moved his hands from the shoulder to her breast. But with a smooch, he undressed her and wore his shirt back.

"Smartass." She giggles.

"Nah, your's better." He said smiling and left her home.

At the class, Richard was playing a better game than before. Though he never defeated the master, he did defeat many other students there.

"What's the matter, son? You look a little... dizzy." Master said, moving his knight forward.

"It's just... too much work in the office." Richard backed his bishop to protect it from the knight.

"None of us are kids here. And you are forgetting, chess is not just about planning your next move. It's very important to read another person so as to predict his next move." Master moved his queen and attacked Richard's bishop with it.

"Yes, so I just came here after making love with my fiancé. How does it affect my game?" Richard randomly asked moving his knight forward.

"Oh! It affects," Master exclaimed and continued while moving his knight. "In a casual game, it's a very effective move to confuse the opponent by talking about their personal life. In this way, the opponent loses his concentration and often plays random tricks, without even thinking twice. Just like you ignored my knight while concentrating on my queen." As he placed his knight and said, "Checkmate."

"How? Oh... I can't move anywhere else. Thanks! I am going to use this trick next time."

"All the best then. Just don't forget to tell people who taught you chess." Master said and he nodded.

Then the amazing weekend for Richard ended and the next day, he was back in his hectic lifestyle. Just a regular day that starts with sighting Deborah smoking alone down the office. Meeting his colleague, his close friend Idhaya and boss Shree, who quite recently made Richard's life a little less hell than what it was before.

An hour later, as he was with his colleague, he saw Deborah going back down and coming back within a few minutes. He guessed she might have gone for smoking again. Then again, she was seen going back and forth for like five times in two hours. He anticipated something was wrong with her as only her makeup was the one thing left which was lifting her face up. The sixth time when she was on her way down, Richard's curiosity just crossed the line and he decided to talk to her. He followed her down the floor on the stairs which was dedicated only to smokers.

"You want to take a puff?" Deborah asked him as he approached her with a look of doubt.

"No! I told you I don't smoke."

"You did? Well, I must have forgotten. And if you don't smoke then don't be here, it's for smokers."

"A place for smokers or the dead souls?" Richard mocked her, but this time she didn't take this as a joke.

"Ugg... A person can't even smoke in peace anymore." Deborah was annoyed with his silly comment. And anyway, being frustrated she threw her cigarette on the floor and after crushing with her feet, she started to walk ahead.

"Deborah! I was just having a casual conversation right now. Why are you being so cranky today?" He said as she reached the door to the office.

"Today? You mentioned Deborah being a bitch before. Then what difference does it make if the bitch is cranky or not?" She then slammed the door on her way in. While Richard was confused.

"What the fuck was that?"

Chapter 13

Rising sunset

It has been two weeks now since Deborah and Abhishek ended their not-so-loving relationship. And how is she holding? Pretty well. Nothing has affected her work. She might be a little dizzy because of her cigarettes, apart from that, not even a tear left her emotional closet. She is sometimes arrogant with people, maybe a little more than usual. But people have already got used to with her behaviour. Her breath sometimes smelled like ashes of her heart. A heart that was believed to be cold is burning high in flames. At that point, the cigarette just felt like a cover up for all the smoke her heart did. Was she fine? Yeah, she was fine, fine for all the eyes that stared her.Except for one.

The one guy, who stood in a line between being a friend and a stranger, Richard Buthello. He was somehow able to look inside her. Maybe, it was because he discerned his feelings of hate turning into sympathy for her. There was a time when he wanted to see her suffer but now when that is happening, he couldn't help himself for being sorry.

At the end of the day, walking down from his office, he spotted Deborah smoking. Well, it wasn't that difficult those days. You just had to look around and there she is, smoking. One hand on a cigarette and another one on her blue umbrella.

He was pretending to walk casually, as he reached close to her. But stopped and before even he could say a word, she said. "Came back to interrupt me?"

"I was not... going to... eh." He stammered.

"You just can't let me smoke in peace, can you?"

"Well, quite frankly, you don't seem to be in peace lately." He said and she stopped puffing.

"That must have made your day better I suppose." She was back to her bitch mode but he just chuckled. She looked at him in surprise.

"Your words don't hurt me anymore." He said.

"That is new for me. But... it soon will." She said, throwing the remains of the cigarette away.

"No, it won't. I know you now." Richard was confident.

"You know nothing about my life." She faced away.

"No! Not your life. But your nature, in quite literal words, you just act like a bitch so that others won't bully."

"Oh! Shut up, Richard." She exclaimed.

"You used to be nice, Maybe a long time ago. Then something happened that made you hate people." Richard said and Deborah looked straight into his eyes. There was an awkward silence between them.

"I am going home, bye." She said and walked towards the parking zone.

"I don't have a ride today, care to give me a lift?" Richard said.

"I hate you a lot." She giggled, "You can either stalk me or wait here till I bring my car here."

"Um... I will wait... On second thought. Stalking is so much fun." And then he joined her in a silent stroll. Their ride started as the dusk began. After a few minutes of silence, he asked her, "Do you know where I live?"

"Eh... Airoli?"

"This is Airoli! Come on, you had no idea where I live, then where were you taking me?" He laughed.

Then after a random chit-chat, he asked, "We are stuck in traffic and I am terribly bored. So, anytime soon you can start your story?"

"This is not the right place for that."

"So, there is a story. See, I knew it" He was curiously excited as he jumped up the seat.

"You want to know my story?" She asked, raising her left eyebrow.

"Affirmative."

"Then we have to take a right turn."

"Right turn? Why? That leads to Belapur. It's so far away."

"Yes, you asked for it. Now don't be a bitch and just enjoy the ride." She said speeding up on the highway to Belapur.

Richard was really exhausted and so he nods off and after an hour of the drive, they reached the place. Suddenly the road became rough and he woke up. He was all dizzy at first, but as soon as his sight got clear, he said.

"Where the hell have you brought me?"

"Just wait."

"There is no light. What is this place." He got a little scared.

"Are you scared Richard?" She teased him.

"No! A little. But that's natural." He said then she stopped her car near a tree.

"It's a fucking jungle out here. Why did you stop?" Richard asked.

"You wanted to know my story, here it starts."

"Here? What were you, Sister of Tarzan? And where is this place? Seriously! Where are we?" He was literally scared of the darkness and silence.

"Just follow me." She said walking down the way to the dense forest.

"Why are you going there? Stupid come back... Fuck!" He said and eventually, he paced up to her following her lead. And then finally they reached.

"Oh wow! This is so damn beautiful. Where are we right now? What's this place called?"

"Broken bridge, Cbd Belapur."

"We are still in Belapur! Damn, how haven't I known about this place until now? Man, I am going to bring Marina here."

"Marina? It's good she is the first person that comes into your mind whenever you see something beautiful. She is really lucky." Deborah said.

"Thanks, but this right now, what you are saying is really scary. What the hell is happening to you right now. How could you speak so sweet? I don't believe it. I can't." Richard said and she laughed.

"Holy shit, you can laugh. Am I dreaming? I think I am still in the car sleeping. This is all just a dream." Richard was sceptical of the recent change of behaviour.

"Does this look like a dream for you? Dark night, cloudy sky with just a hint of moonlight. Standing on a river bank surrounded by no one but just trees and sand. And the sound of water tinkling that broken bridge?" She said staring at a small narrow bridge which was half submerged under the water. "Can your dream be so real?"

"This is not a dream. I can't imagine you at this place. How often do you come here?"

"Often? I suppose after a decade; I am coming here."

"A decade?"

"Hmm... I hate this place how much I love it." She said, taking out the packet of cigarette out of her purse.

"Oh, come on. I thought you were happy here. Why do you have to smoke again?" Richard asked.

"Do you want one?" She said, showing him the packet.

"I told you before that I don't smoke." Richard said.

"You did, but I don't trust anyone." She said.

"Huh! Don't tell this to anyone." He said, picking up one cigarette.

"Tell anyone? Whom do I have to even share anything in life? You stupid fuck."

"Yeah, so shall we start your story?"

"My story?" She said and after taking a puff she continued, "Thanks for taking me back in time. Back when I was weak and..." She started being sarcastic, but then what she said kept blowing Richard's mind. They both were smoking up against the breeze with a story she said that sounded like the sad tales.

Chapter 14

Rose once blossomed

A girl with hairs long till her back. Fair skin and eyes brown. Skinny body, yet she looked stunning because of her maintained figure. She had the book of 11th grade's accounts on her lap. As she was studying, she received an unknown call on her Nokia flip phone.

"Hello." She said.

"Eh... I think your boyfriend is cheating on you." His voice was too sloppy. "What? Dude, who the hell are you to say like that?" She asked angrily.

"I am not joking. He is cheating on you for a very long time. In fact, he is with another girl right now." This time he sounded firm.

"No... That's impossible. I don't believe you. I don't even know you but are you sure you are calling the right person. I mean you might be calling someone else but called me so that means my boyfriend is not cheati..." As she was speaking in a gloomy voice, he interrupted.

"You are Deborah D'mello right?"

"Hmm... yes"

"Then I am calling the right person. And if you still don't believe me then let me prove it to you. I know where they are now." He said. Out of curiosity, she instantly agreed to go out with a complete stranger. Also, twelve years back, she was quite a different person than what we know by now. She would easily trust anyone and was nice to everyone.

Deborah got ready to leave in five minutes. Which was the quickest of all time. She had to wait fifteen minutes before that guy made an appearance. He also looked like a college student who came on a bike. She was not sure whom to look for, but he was certain about her. He parked right in front of her and said.

"Hi Deborah, we spoke on the phone." The guy said.

"Yes, let's go." Without even thinking much she got on the bike with a complete stranger. They didn't speak much except for asking how much further. And after almost an hour she started to suspect something. As their route left out of the city into a rural area. Trees surround the road and also acted as a cover from the sun.

"What is this place?" Deborah asked.

"We are at Belapur." He replied.

"So far from Airoli!" Her heart pumped rapidly.

"Yeah, he is here only. You would see, soon enough."

"But how have I come so far with a stranger? I don't even know your name."

"Yeah, sorry about that. Actually, I was waiting for you to ask, but you were a little distracted so I didn't bother. By the way, I am Vipul."

"Hmm." She got too anxious as well as scared. Like it was a big mistake to trust a stranger. Then he stopped his bike near a bushy region with no one around.

"Why did you stop?" She asked.

"We reached." He replied and she instantly stepped back the moment she got off the bike.

"Hey, you can trust me. I am going to prove it to you, just come with me once." Vipul said.

"But how do you know him and me as well?

"Eh... I am his friend."

"What? Then why would you do that to him?" Deborah was shocked.

"Because I think whatever he is doing is not right. And I just want to help you." He convinced her to walk with him in the jungle. It wasn't exactly a jungle, just some trees on the way, but for Deborah, it was one. She had never been to any place other than a mall before. She was still in the suspicion that something is not right and she should run back immediately if he tries to do anything. But the moment the jungle ended, she saw a place so beautiful to believe it is in Belapur. It was like a seashore, but was a river surrounded by trees on both the side of the water body. And a narrow bridge made of wood going across the river halfway.

"What is this place?" She asked.

"It's called broken bridge." He replied and then he pointed towards her left on a bushy region. She saw a guy making out with someone. When she walked close to them, she burst into tears.

"How could you do this to me? You said you loved me, and you will marry me. How? And why Jay?"

Jay was her boyfriend whose hands were wandering above another girl's breast at the moment. "No no... it's not like that. Wait... how did you come here?" Then when he saw Vipul, he understood that he brought her here. "Vipul what the fuck are you doing?"

He didn't utter a word. Even the girl with Jay was confused as to what is going on. But Deborah was too much heartbroken as he was her first love. She couldn't stand a sight of them, so she walked away. Vipul paced up to her and tried to calm her. Eventually, she was calm as they walked out of the jungle holding onto each other. She was the damsel in distress at that place. And he put all the efforts that he could to keep her heart from shattering into pieces as they walk out of that place.

Then he dropped her outside her building and only saying a "Thank you." She walked with a heavy heart. Later that night she received a call, it was of Jay. He went on for hours convincing her how wrong he was doing something like this to her. He begged on the phone to give her one last chance. And he promised to never cheat on her again. She was so naïve she believed him and accepted him again.

She was Just 16 years old back then while Jay was 19. He was in the same college studying B.com 2nd year while she was in her 11th-grade commerce. Their relationship was back to normal. Going to a movie theatre and other places where they could get some privacy. But after a few weeks with the help of Vipul, she again found out that he was cheating on her again.

"I hate you. I can't be with you anymore." Deborah was alone in Jay's house. She came there as soon as she got a call from Vipul. He told her that he was with Jay last night and later Jay left the party with another girl.

"Listen, Debo... You don't understand this."

"Don't understand what?" She said in disgust.

"I am older than you." Jay said.

"You didn't have any problem with that the first time we kissed."

"But listen, we just kissed and that's all we do each time we make out. I can't handle that; I have needs, desperate needs and you won't have sex with me. Then how could I be happy with you even if I love you?"

"We talked about this before. I am young, very young. Just for you, I agreed to have sex after 18 and still you can't wait for two years. You said you loved me and then too..."

"No, I can't. You don't know how it feels. I am so much frustrated because of this. Because of you."

"Please don't say that. I love you, but I am not ready now." Deborah hesitated as he came close to her and started kissing her by the neck. Unlike other times she couldn't resist his hands going down her belly. She was lost in love and lost her virginity in it.

Deborah said this to Richard as they both were puffing Cigarette on the broken bridge. "That's harsh. But is it the end or is there more to your past?" Richard asked, throwing the remains of his cigarette away.

"End? This was not even an interval. It was just a trailer you could say." Deborah said and removed more two cigarettes from the packet.

"I don't smoke this much. We can just talk."

"Yes, but we got a lot more to talk so just take it."

"Alright. So, what happened next? I can anticipate very well, but you go ahead."

"Hmm... What would happen next? He had sex with me a few more times and all those times I never knew he actually was serious with someone else. Glad Vipul was there to expose him and eventually, Jay left me when he was bored with me."

"That's what I anticipated." Richard proudly said raising his cigarette. Deborah gazed at him angrily and he was back to the serious mode.

"Well, I was fine. I did cry a lot, but still fine as I realized he wasn't the one for me. But I was not fine with this rumour spreading out in the college that I am a whore."

"People knew about it?" Richard asked.

"Of course they knew. Before, I was considered as a studious student, but by the end of 11th grade. I got names like slut and hooker. A girl who would easily have sex with anyone in love." She made a poker face.

"Then did you change your college?"

"I was about to change. Until one day when I met this guy. This really sweet guy from my college. He was in 12th grade, again another older guy but I knew he was different. His name was Sky." And with another cigarette, she continued her story.

Chapter 15

Strong heart because it became cold

Sky, Handsome boy of the college. Who looked too decent with no beard, not even a moustache. Quite outspoken and also flirtish. That's how he was, or you could say how he wanted others to think he was.

One day when Deborah was shopping with her mother in a supermarket. She saw Sky there who was also shopping but was not alone. He was with a girl, who kept Sky on her tail. Following her everywhere, Dominating all the way. Deborah has seen Sky many times in the college. He was quite an extrovert person, like the one who leads people. It was the first time when she saw him following someone. She found it cute to see the other side of Sky.

While she was staring him, he glanced her and she got scared. Quickly she looked away and hid behind the shelf of chocolate. Her heart was pumped up after a very long time. And at that moment she got a crush on Sky. On that day, she decided to give another chance to her college and her heart too.

The next day in college, when she entered her classroom, she got surprised to see Sky there. He was talking with the class representative. But all the time they both kept on exchanging awkward stares with each other. They were sharing a unique bond already in the wind without having a single word. Then all of a sudden he left the room unspoken. Later that day, when she was outside the college waiting for her car to arrive, she saw Sky walking by her side. Without hesitating even, a bit she stopped him.

"Hi, Sky." She said.

"Hi, Deborah." He replied, then there was an awkward silence between them.

"It's weird we both know each other's name even after not having a single conversation ever." She blushed.

"No, it's ok. I mean we both are famous in college." He chuckled and her face went pale.

"No, listen, I didn't mean to say that. I was just trying to continue the conversation. I swear!" Sky added.

"Hmm..." She just looked down in shame. Then her car approached. The driver parked it right next to her. She was about to leave, then he stopped her holding her hands.

"Deborah, I am extremely sorry if I had hurt you. And no, I don't think of you the way others think. Trust me, I am not lying." He said and she just nodded. Then he continued.

"Hmm... I still feel bad about this. I want to make up to you. What can I do?" He asked and she just stared him in a question mark.

"Alright, what if I take you to a movie tomorrow, after college?" Sky asked and with an expressionless face, she replied in a numb voice "Ok." And got in her car. He was surprised, eyes popped out a little and both eyebrows up. The fact that she instantly agreed to go out with him made quite a loose as well jolly image of her to him. He waved saying "Bye take care." While she waved back with a smile. The moment car left that street her feeling burst like a cracker with a thousand smiles struggling to come out at once. That was the best thing that ever happened to her in a very long time.

The next day, they went to a movie skipping the last few lectures of the college. But in the theatre, they didn't actually see the movie. Instead, all they did was talk. And most of their conversation didn't even make any sense. They just didn't want to stop hearing each other's voices.

After a few days, things changed. They talked every day on the phone. It was the time when WhatsApp wasn't a thing yet and text messages were limited to only hundreds. Which was nothing in comparison to how much they spoke. But in so many talks one day it was personal. The day he made a confession. That confession changed the status of her relationship with him. As he revealed that he is in love. Unfortunately, he was in love with Samaira. Samaira, the girl who was with him at the mall the first time they saw each other. And she realized her relationship with him changed from friends to best friends. The line she could never cross, Friendzone.

Deborah was Sky's only best friend while he was her second-best friend on her list. Soon another rumour spread out in the college and this time it was done by her friend herself, Nikita. The rumour was that Sky and Deborah were dating but in fact, they used to go out to movies, lunch and some other places. But they weren't dating. This was affecting their friendship which she couldn't let happen. So, she stopped talking to Nikita and not just her but also other girls from her college.

Well, it didn't help much because one-day Sky himself told her that they need to stop talking. It was affecting his relationship with Samaira. On that day, she was done hiding her feelings. It wasn't the easiest of course, as she broke into tears when she said, "I love you Sky."

He didn't give an answer to that, but yeah, he also couldn't let her cry. Hugged her from behind comforting her until she stopped. And finally, he kissed her on the forehead and left. Apparently, things changed quickly after that. She became very vulnerable to him, and he kept her as an open option. From forehead, his lips went lower and lower, but their relationship remained the same. She let him use her whenever he needed to, do whatever she wanted just with a feeling that one day they would be together. In a fantasy world, she lived in for the next 6 months. But her world soon collapsed when Sky convinced her that he got Samaira pregnant. It became her worst nightmare. She always knew that he was double dating. She knew because he himself told her that, but with a fake promise that he is not serious with her and soon would be committed to Deborah. That was the last time she ever came into a relationship with anyone. Richard was speechless to hear this side of Deborah.

"I don't have any words to support you. I am shocked." Richard said.

"Really? You are shocked already?" She said looking at him and puffing.

"Wait! Is there more?" He exclaimed and asked ahead.

"Sky may have been my second-best friend and my love, but there was someone closest to me in my past. My first best friend, Vipul!"

"Vipul? Should I expect something bad here too?" He asked and she chuckled then continued.

"Vipul was with me all the time from Jay to Sky. In those two years, I adapted his habit of smoking. But in secrecy. I couldn't let it spread out like another rumour that I was a smoker."

"I understand tha..."

"Don't interrupt again." She said and he shrugged, then kept smoking while she continued her story. Another part of her past, the only one which didn't spread as a rumour.

Vipul was the only person she was close to. They almost shared everything with each other. They didn't have any secrets between them, but they maintained each other's secret very well. And the broken bridge was their favourite place. It was their spot for smoking and drinking. As time passed from Jay to Sky, Vipul had been always single.

One day, which was in time after the scene of Sky ended. Deborah and Vipul were in the theatre watching a lame movie. The theatre was almost empty and in that dark atmosphere, he lost himself.

"Deborah." He said in a dreamy voice.

"Hmm?"

"I want to kiss you." He said.

"You are ok, Right?" She chuckled.

"I am sorry." He said. "It's okay, it happens. Forget it." She said, but after a few minutes, he said again.

"I really want to kiss you."

"Shut up now." She hesitated. Then he took her hands and started kissing it.

"I don't like it Vip. Please stop it!" She exclaimed, but he didn't stop and went to her neck. She tried holding him back but was too strong for her. He kept on kissing on the neck and groping until she finally pushed him away. It was clear from her face that she was upset. He got scared at that moment and leaned back.

"Oh no... I don't know what I was doing. I am sorry. Really... Please, I am sorry. Try to understand it just happened."

"Listen, Vipul, don't ever talk about this. Ever again." Deborah didn't even look at his face. While he kept mumbling to himself. "I am sorry, sorry, sorry."

"Hey, just stop. I have forgotten about it." She said and he nodded then he asked.

"Are we still friends?"

"Of course, we are, you are the only friend I have. How can I lose you?" She said with a smile and things went back to normal.

She literally forgave him regardless of what he did. He didn't lose her trust and they kept on smoking and drinking as usual.

Almost a month later, they were at their favourite spot, the broken bridge, smoking cigarettes. They sat on the cliff of the bridge, with his hands on her shoulder. But after a few puffs, his hands lowered down to her waist and then to her breast. She instantly caught it and kept it back on her shoulder with a humming voice.

But that didn't stop him and again, his hands went down to her boobs. His hand got firm and intention spoiled. Throwing his cigarette away, he stopped her from one hand and while groping from another. Her cigarette fell on the river while she was resisting. But she was as delicate as dandelion and could not stop him. He kept on harassing as his hands went down to her vagina and his lips locked on hers. She didn't even try to scream as the place was solitary and she was too scared of his action. Eventually, he asked angrily "Why aren't you kissing back?"

"Vipul, please don't do this. I beg you please stop."

"What's wrong with you. It's just for one time that's all."

"No, I cannot do this."

"Why can't you? You did it with others then why not me." He said and continued kissing her neck.

Then finally, she behaved bravely and pushed him completely away saying.

"When did you become like this? I won't let you touch me anymore." She said standing up and walked away from the cliff. He followed her and as she reached the shore, he stopped her. She was standing by a wooden rod.

"Listen, I am lusting on you."

"From when?" She asked.

"The truth is that the reason I told you about Jay's another girlfriend was because I wanted to get close to you."

"What the fuck are you talking about?" Deborah got goosebumps.

"But that time was different. It was in the past."

"And you never thought about it anytime before. About doing me?" She was angry.

"I... Eh... I did. A lot every time to be honest. But I tried to control myself. I just can't control anymore. Let's have sex just once. And I promise things will be back to normal."

"Vipul, just stop this bullshit. Just look at you. What kind of person are you?"

"Oh really... So you won't have sex with me?" He was intimidating.

"No...! Never." She said and he pushed her so hard that her sleeves caught on the wooden rod and torn as she fell down. He said fuck off on her face and left on his bike leaving her helpless as she cried. She pulled herself together and started walking in shame. Her right sleeve got torn till her waist and because of which her bra was visible. And everyone in that village area stared her, but no one stepped up to even provide a piece of clothing.

Eventually, she found a bus and reached the city. Bought a jacket from a shop and wore it before reaching home.

"Did you buy that jacket to avoid your parents knowing what happened?" Richard asked and she replied.

"Yes, of course. But no matter how much I tried I couldn't hide my emotions from my parents. I cried a lot every day. Without even sharing this incident. They asked me to even see a psychiatrist, but I refused. Months passed and never saw Vipul again. Because of all this, I got average grades in spite of being a scholar. But out of all this, the worst part was that I was upset all the time not because of what Vipul did but because I lost my only friend. My best friend. It sometimes feels like I never really had any friend or someone to trust."

"Then what happened?" Richard asked.

"You expect more tragedies in my life?"

"No, I just asked... Eh... Well."

"Well... After my 12th got over here. I begged my father to send me away, and he tried with all his efforts. Because of which I got admission in an institute of management in Paris. Didn't even dare to make any friends there. Just adapted their lifestyle and clothing by observing them. And yeah, had sex a couple times, but without any attachment. Only the time I needed and not the other way around. Never the other way around. Soon I was back in India after my graduation got completed and since then for almost seven years I have been working here in iHNS. I did have casual relationships before, but they all ended."

"I suppose one ended very recently. If I am not wrong." Richard asked.

"Yes, yes it did. I was with Abhishek. He is a young, college going guy from my building." She said and he teetered.

"What? It's my life and my choice." Deborah glared him.

"I am sorry. And not just sorry for this, but also everything else too. I mean I always thought of you as a bad person and said bad things to you in the face..." As he was speaking, she interrupted saying. "You mean calling me a bitch?"

"Yeah, that only. But my point is I never knew what you went through before and that's the only reason I acted like that. You are really strong actually..." As he was speaking, she again interrupted.

"Richard, it's getting late. I think, so we should leave. Though you can still continue it in the car."

She said and they both left. Talked a lot on their way back home. Then by 9 pm, she dropped him outside her complex and drove away.

"What the fuck! Was that Richard with Deborah?" Said Deeksha inside her car in the opposite lane. Marina nodded being baffled.

"Should I still drop you at his home?" Deeksha asked and she shook her head.

"Hey, don't cry now. He is not worth it." She said and they too drove away.

Chapter 16

All about yesterday

"What's wrong with you? I mean, why are you behaving like this today?" Richard was worried as he had never seen this face of her in all these times. It was scary for him, as that expression of her felt revengeful. Like something is coming to hunt him. A prospect of misery. That's everything Richard deducted from the cheerful face of Deborah.

"How am I behaving?" She smiled without any restraint.

"You got any plans to ruin my life? Is that what's making you happy?" He asked jokingly and she chuckled.

"This is so weird. I don't see anything devilish or horns around your head." He continued and she kept on laughing Joyously. But soon her smile faded as she bit her lips and eyelids flickered saying.

"I am sorry."

"Eh... Can you say that again? I forgot to record this moment in my camera..."

"Richard, you are never getting that again."

"I am just joking and yeah. You are forgiven."

"You didn't even ask me why I was sorry, forgiven what then?"

"I suppose you are sorry for being a bitch to me all this time." He teased her and continued typing a mail.

"No, I am not sorry for that... and if I was a bitch to you, you were no less than a bastard to me either." She smirked and he nodded sniggering. Then the mood of joyfulness was gone as she got angry at Richard for taking her small talks for granted.

"I am finally, happily like a friend, talking to you and bro! You don't even give a shit." She said and he startled as he looked at her.

"Eh... eh... I am sorry. It's just a work, a lot of work and I am stressed."

"Yeah, you look like a Monday morning on Tuesday." She said and lightens up.

"Why were you sorry anyway?" Richard asked while continuing typing his email.

"Yeah, well. Do you need to know that? Everything is better between us, you really want to spoil this with the truth."

"Quit whining. Just say it."

"Well, the reason you are all stressed up with work is that of me."

"No! It's because of this fucking company." Richard exclaimed.

"Are you sure about that?" Deborah asked politely.

"Yeah, Shree told me. I had to do overtime; it's the company's order."

"Hmm, well, in that case, I am Shree's company." She said and he laughed. Then she gave him a dirty look, and Richard took some sense out of her statement.

"Wait... Are you telling me that, he gave me so much burden of work because you told him to?" Richard was shocked.

"Don't take this personally. The situation was..." As she was speaking Richard interrupted.

"Yeah, why would I take it personally? You are the reason why I am doing over time for almost a month..."

"At that time..."

"It's September now, and if you hadn't told me this then how many more months would I have been like this?" He appeared to be angry.

"I am extremely sor..." Her face turned pale so he softened a bit.

"Relax, I am just kidding. I am not angry." Richard said cheering up.

"What the fuck!" Deborah exclaimed and continued, "You know, I thought I lost your company just now."

"Nope, not so soon. Come on we just started talking from yesterday and you think I am going to sabotage it over some past?"

"I don't know how your brain works."

"Anyway, does that mean, I don't have to do overtime anymore? Can you please talk a way out of this?" He asked desperately.

"I am here for seven years. I have a command so of course, I can help you in this case."

"Thank God!" He put his palm on his face, "I am so revealed... ugh." He mourned.

"You sound weird." She said and they chuckled.

"Hey, how did you convince Shree to do this?" Richard asked.

"I am Deborah D'mello, I think, that's enough to say." She was confident.

"So what? You had sex with him?"

"What? Fuck no! Richard, you all men are the same." She said standing up.

"No! Where are you going now?" He asked as she walked towards the door.

"To help you out with Shree." She sneered at him and continued, "Also, I am a manager, I don't have much free time, bye."

"Bye..." He smiled and continued working on his laptop.

In Shree's cabin, when Deborah entered and walked all to way to be seated, Shree just kept glaring her.

"What do you want now?" He asked.

"A little bit help."

"What kind of?"

"Something related to Richard." The moment she said this he became helpless as he said.

"No please, I already made his work hell. I can't do it anymore. I feel guilty for it."

"Relax... It's the other way round. Free Richard, no more overtime or burden. Make everything back to normal. Make it all go away." She said and he got stunned.

"What?" Shree asked, still staying stunned.

"Do it!"

"Why are you playing with people's life, Deborah?" Shree was concerned.

"Well, that's the point here. I am not playing anymore, alright? Just do what I said and I will even delete the voice conversation that I had with you."

"Ah..." He said breathing out. And as she was walking out, he said.

"So, I just wanted to ask this. What are you doing tonight?"

"Hmm?"

"Eh... I was saying. After the shift is done. Would you like to have coffee with me? Just for old time's sake." He was nervous.

"When did we ever went for a coffee?"

"No!" breathing heavily, he continued to stammer, "It's only... Eh... Mm coffee, like..."

"Why a coffee, so that you could end up in bed with me?" She replied straight staring into his eyes.

"Wow... Well, that's not what I meant. But that sounds more like a conclusion to this date... Eh... Coffee meet." He said and she chuckled.

"Hey, did you record this time again?" He got tensed.

"I don't know, maybe. Goodbye Shree." She said and left while he smashed his head into the desk.

At evening, Richard was escorting Deborah to her car. "Are you really not going to smoke at all today?" Richard asked.

"Probably not! Thought a little change would be good." Deborah replied.

"Yes, it is great."

"And one more thing... Mmm... Thanks for yesterday." She said and he stared her in amusement.

"Are you sure that you are alright? First sorry and now thank you. This is certainly not you. It feels like I am walking with someone else." He said and she giggled.

"I bet you have never listened to such a tragic story before?" She asked, and he scratched his head while nodding.

"What was that?" Deborah asked.

"What? Nothing..."

All about yesterday

"No, it isn't nothing. Just say it or you won't be working here again." She warned him.

"Seriously! Stop with this heavy talk. Anyway, the thing is your past was really really heartbreaking but..."

"But what?"

But it's common." He said and she stopped strolling.

"Common? Like these things happen to every girl." Deborah said.

"No, not every girl, but... Already two of my college friends had something similar. One was even molested by a cousin. So, it was nothing new to hear. In fact, it wa..." He stopped when he saw a week-old Deborah coming back again.

"No! I can't deal with grumpy you again."

"I am not angry." She faked a smile, then continued, "Huh... Fuck it. Currently, none of them would be doing better than me."

"Yeah right, none of them is a manager or anything. One even got married and she is a housewife now."

"So typical! I am still the great Deborah D'mello."

"Yes, you are. Well, my bike is over there."

"And my car's here, bye."

"Yeah, bye." They shook hands and left.

Later, at Richard's home. They both were smoking joints.

"Marina's going to kill me for this." Richard said staring his joints.

"She's going to kill us both for this. I am the one spoiling my elder brother." Matthew said and they laughed.

"By the way, how was your date last night?" Matthew asked and Richard's face shook.

"What date?"

"Marina called me earlier last night. She asked me to come home late. She said something like you were stressed so she is going to surprise you and... fuck you." He ended up laughing.

"Shut up. But she never showed up."

"Really! Earlier, when I came you were sleeping. So, I thought you got laid."

"No, I didn't. I was just tired with... Eh... This work thing."

"Hmm... Alright." Matthew said, passing him the joint. "Alright..." He said, puffing up.

Dark thunderstruck stormy night, dim blue seductive lights, clothes all around the room and warm hands grabbed the boobs as she keeps on mourning, "Ah... Fuck! Ah..." Finally, the bed stopped shaking and the room got silent with only the noise of heavy breathing. Deborah said, looking into his eyes, "You are great in the sack! Seriously, it was the best sex I had after a long time."

"Ah... You were fucking ravishing too, Deb..." Said Shree getting back on top of her. And the night continued with the pain of pleasure.

Chapter 17

Wine, the best solution.

Swirling dead red leaf flew in the cold breeze. That breeze took the leaf on a tiny adventure of winds until the moment it got stuck by a burning cigarette. Flares of tiny flame blew up in the air as the leaf takes cigarette down with it, only to end it from growing any further.

"Fuck, that was the only cigarette left." Deborah got distressed.

"See, even God is giving you a message. Slow down your smoking habit. It will affect your health." Richard advised.

"Oh! Wise words from a smoker."

"Hey, don't say it in public." He was a little paranoid.

"Richard, there's no one around." Deborah said as there were only cars passing by the road.

"Still, you can never let this out, that I smoke." He said, and she replied in a sarcastic funny voice.

"Yeah! I got it, teenage boy."

"You don't understand commitment, do you?"

"If you really were that committed, then you wouldn't be smoking it in the first place." Deborah said, turning around and started walking saying, "Bye Richard."

"Wait... I am coming with you." Richard said, jumping ahead of her.

"Where? To my home?"

"No... Someplace else just come there with me."

"Ok, first of all, I am too exhausted today. I had the worst meeting of my life at the conference room and secondly, we are not going at Belapur now. It's far and I am in no mood of driving that long..." She even looked tired as her shirt was creased and eyes dangling.

"No! We are not going there and you don't have to drive. I will drive."

"Alright, I will be standing right here." She said handing over the keys. He then went towards the parking lot. After a few minutes he came back with her car, parked it outside the façade of iHNS building and looked for her but she was nowhere to be found. Then all of a sudden, she just dropped off his back standing on the other side of the door.

"Where were you, I was looking for you?" Richard asked.

"I went searching for you, was wondering what's taking you so long. Where were you?"

"I had some problem getting out of the lot. Never mind, shall we go now?" Richard asked, opening the door on his side.

"Let's go."

Wine, the best solution.

The atmosphere was pleasant with trees shedding their leaves, covered the whole ground in its maroon blanket. Like the frost on an ice cream, leaves on the streets. The third week of September, autumn, it indeed was beautiful. Richard and Deborah were walking in the bed of nature at the Driving Range, Kharghar.

"I agree, this place is beautiful. But I can't take it anymore." Deborah was hyperventilating when the steep slope felt like rock climbing to her.

"Now you see how your health is getting affected because of smoking?" Richard teased.

"Just shut up and sit here." She said as she got down on the muddy floor of the hill they were climbing.

"You are sitting down! On the ground! This really is a miracle." He said and she gave him a dirty look.

"Anyway, just look at this place, isn't it beautiful to see the whole city orange under the rays of the setting sun, even that golf course looks golden. How magnificent God made this world and we don't even admi..." As he was speaking, he got shocked when he turned and looked at Deborah "Oh! What the hell!" He exclaimed.

"What?" She said, picking out a cigarette from her new packet full of it.

"You said that was the last cigarette back at the office, how did you get a new one right now?" Richard asked.

"While you were getting my car out, I bought a new packet of cigarette. Besides this view, Richard I live on the 18th floor. I practically see it every day. Buildings, a bunch of mountains, sunrise and sunset everything from my window." She said and he made a poker face.

"Yeah! I do too, but it is different here. Outside with friends, that's more fun." He said taking a cigarette from her.

"Friends? Is that what we are now?" She asked and lit her cigarette.

"Yes! Unfortunately." He chuckled.

"By the way, how do you know this place? Is it your secret place of you and Marina?"

"No, Idhaya told me about it. She and her fiancé sometimes visit this place after office." Richard said.

"Who's Idhaya now? Sounds like I know her?" She asked, taking a puff and they continued talking until sunset.

Later by 7 at evening, when Richard got home, he saw Marina's shoe in the shoe rack. He walked inside with a smile thinking she came here to surprise him. But when he saw her face, he just couldn't figure out what was going on. Frowned face, eyes under the shadow of tears and dry lips, sat Marina in black jeans and blue top.

"Hi, honey! What a surpri..." As he was walking with a smile Matthew blocked him, holding his shoulder and said.

"Richard, brother, there's something we should talk about now." But Matthew's eyes already said that Richard is in trouble. Richard sat on the chair opposite to Marina.

Wine, the best solution.

"What's going on? And why haven't you replied to my texts in like two days?" Richard asked being perplexed.

"So, you did notice something was wrong, couldn't even care to call?" She asked and his voice went numb.

"Say something Richard." She asked.

"Yes, what's wrong? And Matthew can you go out somewhere else?"

"No! He stays right here, I need him." Marina was stubborn with her actions. Richard just blinked his eyes for a second before uttering another word.

"Whassup?" He said acting casual.

"Really smooth brother." Matthew added.

"Just stay out of it bro." Richard said.

"Bro, she knows."

"Knows what? There's nothing to hide!" Richard exclaimed.

"She knows about you and Deborah." Matthew said and again Richard went speechless for a while. Which made him look even more guilty.

"This is surely a misunderstanding cause there is noth..." As Richard was speaking Marina interrupted.

"Two days ago, on 19 September at 10 in the night, I saw you and Deborah outside this building." She confronted him.

"That's not exactly right."

"Don't tell me I am wrong, don't lie Richard!" She yelled and continued, "I was there, I was going to come over to make love to you, but you fucked me instead." She was damn angry and there Matthew sat in the middle of all this, stuck and uncomfortable.

"Let me explain." He said getting close to her.

"Don't you even dare to touch me. And don't say that it was just overtime, then she dropped you home out of pity."

"Yes, it was overtime. You know I have been doing overtime for a month now." He said in a high pitch.

"So, it's been going on for a month?"

"No, no, no... no what the hell. Matthew just tell her something?" He drifted his topic of discussion, and Matthew added "Eh... He doesn't smoke any... more."

"No, you know everything, tell her there's nothing between me and Deborah." Richard asked and Matthew said, "Yes, I know everything, there's nothing between me... umm... Richard and Deborah." He said while Richard was shaking his and Marina wasn't even pleased.

"No! Come on, just tell her how much I love her." He asked again and Matthew said staying uncomfortable.

"Yes! He loves you... Much... Very much... Yes." He said in a monotonous voice.

"Are you both done or there's more to this act?" Marina asked stepping towards the door.

Wine, the best solution.

"Honey!" Richard rushed to stop her.

"Don't go I love you. And Deborah is the last person you should be worrying about. She is just a friend."

"Still a friend?" Marina asked.

"What?" Richard was sceptical.

"Goodbye, Richard." She said walking out of the door. He stood there with an empty room of thoughts.

Days passed by, as Richard started to ignore Deborah at the office. He knew this was necessary to maintain his relationship with her longtime love Marina. He used to smile and wave whenever he saw her at the office and eventually, after two weeks he completely stopped talking to her. Then one day, on October 1st their office left early. Richard was walking down the stairs and the moment he stepped outside, he saw Deborah in her usual place, smoking. While passing by, as a courtesy he smiled and kept walking.

"That's it?" Deborah asked.

"Huh?"

"You are not going to stop me from smoking?" She asked.

"Eh... No, it's... Your life so..." He was turning back.

"Hey Richard, is everything alright?" Deborah was concerned.

"Yes."

"Stop lying! You haven't been talking to me for quite a few days. Something definitely happened to you."

"I can't talk to you... About it, it's personal." He said and she made a poker face. "Shut up." Deborah said and a started walking saying "Come on."

"Where?"

"Stop asking so many questions and come." She said and for a moment he just stood there blank while she was a few steps ahead. She turned back and raised her left eyebrow. He then took a step forward and eventually went with her. Deborah took Richard to her home. The moment he walked inside his heartbeat pumped up in fear. He was very nervous and said.

"Is this your house?"

She looked at him in bewilderment and said, "Yes, I told you that a few seconds ago."

"Yes, I have never been to... This place before." He said, staring each and every corner of the room.

"You are acting really weird today, the heck is up with you?" She asked, smiling, taking out a bottle of wine, Nine Hills Shiraz rose.

"Nothing..." He said in an abnormally calm way slowly sitting on the couch. She then took two glasses of wine, washed it. Then tucked out her white shirt from black pant to get relaxed as she was home. Then she poured wine on both the glasses and offered one to Richard, who took it with his eyes bugging her face. She then sat on the couch next to Richard and laughed at him.

"This is certainly not what I should be doing." Richard said.

"You are too much tensed up that's why I offered you wine. Take a sip, relax, then we will talk." He said and took a big sip, wait, no. He just finished it in one sip and leaned back relaxing breathing out.

"Look at you, there was a time when I wanted to see you this way, dead from the heart. And now that you are dead I am sympathizing with you, being a friend." She smiled.

"Friend... I am sorry, but we can't be friends anymore." He said.

"What?" She chuckled.

"I am serious, this friendship is affecting my life. My personal life with Marina."

"What do I have to do with Marina?" She was clueless.

"She found out about us? Saw us that day when we went to the broken bridge." Richard said looking at the ceiling.

"Found out what? We are just friends stupid, can't you say that." She said in a high pitch.

"She wouldn't believe me no matter what I say. Now that I stopped talking to you, she at least started talking to me again."

"So that's why you weren't talking to me these few days?" Deborah asked.

"Yes."

"And I thought you were busy or something and couldn't get time to even properly look at me, and I completely understood that." She was getting angry.

"I am sorry."

"Sorry? I thought you were my friend. Unlike you, I don't have a luxury of people whom I can trust. I never had a person in my life in years with whom I could just talk freely for hours without any allegation." As she was saying he interrupted.

"Try to understand."

"No! You try to understand. Richard, I don't trust anyone." Her eyes were scary but lonely, "But you are here, in my house right now. Drinking wine with me alone in a closed room and I am not even worried cause I thought you would never betray me. Turns out you are the worst of all the men I have had in my life. I can't believe you just thought we could be like best friends of two days and then everything will go back to normal."

"I am sor..."

"Stopping saying sorry! God!" She yelled angrily.

"What should I do?" His voice sounded desperate.

"Find a solution and fix this, but I am not losing another friend and only friend I have in my life." She said finishing her wine.

"Wait, there is one thing." He sighed and told her the plan he just came up with.

Wine, the best solution.

"Oh Richard, this is the worst idea ever. Like literally the worst of the worst Idea." She was confident and walked to get the bottle of wine.

"I know, I just made it up or maybe the wine made this plan." He said while she came back with the bottle. Then he raised his glass to her and while she was filling it he asked.

"So, what do you think? Huh... Would you help me?"

After filling it, she sat back on her side of the couch just drank from the bottle itself, leaned back and said "This is going to be a disaster. But still, I am with you on this." And smiled, looking at him and he finally had a light of hope in his smile.

Chapter 18

What do we deserve?

Pleasant aroma like the sea was the odour of Shrimp curry, along with garlic fried rice made it more alluring. Which was served at table 12, side sofa table where sat Richard and Marina to have dinner.

"Mmm..." She said biting the first piece of shrimp.

"Good, isn't it?" Richard asked.

"Delicious." She replied.

"I am glad we are doing this." Richard said.

"Yeah, it's been a long while since we had dinner together."

"I know, it's all my fault. I was busy in my office and then things got weird between us because of de..." As he was speaking Marina interrupted.

"Richard, you don't have to say anything about it now. What all happened is gone, buried. Let's keep it that way. Things are going to be better from now, right?" She asked and he started stammering. Marina was confused to see Richard so nervous. But before asking him what was wrong, she herself went speechless when she saw her.

What do we deserve?

A lady wearing Red gown, shoulderless till her knees, that made her look like she was dipped in red wine to her lips. Hairs short but enough to hide her left eye and a heel, dark maroon. She walked straight to Richard's table and said, "I came."

"Eh... Marina, she's Deborah, Deborah D'mello." Richard said crying in his thoughts. "Why does she have to look more beautiful than my fiancé, just why today."

"Hi, good to... finally, meet you." Deborah tried to be friendly, but Marina ignored her and whispered.

"Richard, What the hell?"

"I will explain everything now." He whispered back.

Deborah saw them both as kids hiding something from their mother. She just called a waiter and made him put on an extra chair to the table. Then she sat there comfortably and said.

"Looks like gonna be a long night, so what are we having?"

"Shrimp, prawns shrimp." Richard said in a low pitch.

Then, with an angry sigh, Marina nodded her head saying, "You can have all of it." folding her hands she glared at Richard. "I am not eating anymore."

"Marina, let's not create a scene here, I just want us to talk and clarify everything. Please, honey." He ended and Deborah tittered. They both Marina and Richard glanced at her.

"What? Ok. Frankly, it's funny to see Richard all melodramatic right now. He's never like this in the office." Deborah said and Marina had a sigh a relief. She at least got a gist that he was never romantic with or even in front of her.

They started eating and stopped talking, literally stopped talking. For a span of 20 minutes, they just concentrated on their plates and communicated through stares. The awkwardness was killing the delicious taste of the food. Then finally, Marina started a normal conversation.

"So, what's going on with your life?"

"It's going quite normal, nothing very special." Deborah replied.

"And how everything going on in your relationship or love life... if there's any?" Marina asked.

"It's also going like the usual." Deborah was losing words.

"Oh, are you in a relationship?" Marina was excited to get the answer she was hoping for. But Deborah got a little anxious and took pause. The situation was getting tensed and then Richard glanced at Deborah, exchanging stares she understood the reference and said.

"Yes, I have been dating Shree for a very long time. Shree is the team leader at our company."

"Tell me more about your love story." She asked.

"Why?" Deborah was getting annoyed.

"Just curious, to know more about your life."

"Then why love life, it's so boring. Can't even think of more words to say about it." Deborah chuckled and Richard added.

"Honey, what she meant was her love life is not so interesting like ours. They are just together for a long time not engaged or true love like ours."

"Oh, you think my love life is boring and not true?" Deborah asked and Richard stared her in confusion.

"Alright, no more love, let's just talk about something else." Marina said.

"How's your normal life going?" Deborah asked Marina.

"My life is going great. Work is on point; health is good by God grace and the best part of my life is Richard. We are engaged and truly happy with each other." Marina said, holding Richard's hands with a smile.

"Pfff..." That's Deborah.

"What did you just do?" Marina got pissed.

"Hmm?"

"You just 'Pff' when I said we are happy together, why did you do that?" Marina asked arrogantly and Richard cried in his thoughts. "Seriously, why did you do that?"

"Huh, it was the food that made me make the sound. Too... Spicy!" Deborah exclaimed and continued eating.

"Hmm... so, eh... how long have you been dating Shree?" Marina came back to her love life and Deborah instantly said. "Two-three weeks."

She didn't realize what she just said until noticed that their table had been quiet for a while. She looked up just to see the faint expressions of betrayal and guilt in either of their faces.

"Oh! I wasn't supposed to say that." Deborah exclaimed.

"Richard, why was she lying? You told her to lie, didn't you? Why do you want her to lie to me?" Marina got angry.

"Marina, it's not at all what you think it is. Just give me a chance to explain once." Richard begged.

"How many more chances you think you deserve?" She asked rhetorically.

"Just one, I'll make everything better. It's just all a misunderstanding..." As Richard was justifying himself, Deborah interrupted "God! This is so cliched."

"No, no no... don't interrupt anymore." Richard said in a low pitch shaking his head.

"Not me but you. Just shut up for a while and let me handle it. You will make it worse." Then Deborah turned towards Marina and continued.

"I frankly can't understand why you are so much worried about Richard being with me. He is just a friend to me, in fact, the only friend I have cause I am not even good at friendship. If you are wondering I might take him away from you then let me make this clear, I don't have feelings, no feelings at all. It has been several years since I have genuinely liked someone. Even my so-called "Relationship." with Shree is nothing but casual... lovemaking. He's anyway married so it's all about casual sex I don't get feelings for anyone." Deborah said.

"Your boyfriend is married to someone else and still you are with him in bed. You don't have any remorse as to how it would affect their relationship." Marina said.

"Out of everything I just said that's all you get?" Deborah asked.

"And you spent time with my fiancé, how casual that is going?"

"You are getting it wrong, so wrong. There could be nothing between Richard and me. I am not even attracted to him in that way." She said and he nodded.

"We just do things that normal friends do, we talk about our day, our jobs, sometimes we drink and smoke. Just the things that friends or colleagues do." Deborah said and Richard lost his breath.

"Smoking? Smoking! No, you cheat, all this time you have... Been... Lying to me..." Marina started hyperventilating. Deborah hit her head with her palm.

"It was nice meeting you Deborah D'mello." she said, gazing Deborah as she gets up and started walking away.

"What the hell! What the hell? The Hell! What should I do now?" Richard was losing his mind.

"Go stop her!" Deborah exclaimed, and he got up. Ran towards to lobby, but it was too late as he saw her car speeding away outside the hotel.

What do we deserve?

Deborah followed up to Richard to the lobby and said. "How fast was she walking?"

"It's no time for a joke!" Richard was serious.

"Hey, relax. You are getting too tense."

"Too tensed? We fucked up. Didn't you just look what just happened?"

"First of all. It's not all my fault. Your plan was fucked up. I mean, you want everything to be cleared and her to know the truth that there's nothing between us. But you want to lie to her even more for her to believe it's true. Just how ironic it sounds, doesn't it?" Deborah said.

"You should have lied. Everything I planned was a lie. Why couldn't you lie?"

"I know how to lie very well. It's just that I don't like making up love stories. That's the one thing I am not good at." She said walking inside.

"Where are you going now?"

"To finish the desert. Aren't you gonna join me?" Deborah asked.

"You think I can eat now?"

"You can either whine about it here like some broken piece of shit or eat it out with a new solution like an adult. Your choice." She said and walked inside and in a moment he followed her to finish the desert.

What do we deserve?

The weekend ended and Monday was on the rocks with coffee in Richard's cabin. He was with the company of his friend cum colleague Idhaya. He told her everything that happened to him, and she couldn't help her to stop laughing out loud.

"This isn't funny Idhaya." Richard said.

"No, it isn't, except for every aspect of it." And she continued.

"Hey, I called you for your help, not to make my life sound like a joke. Which it is right now."

"Hmm... let's see what we can do. This sounds like a mess, but a fixable mess." She had some hopes.

"Really? You think I could save my engagement?"

"I have some sort of similar experience like this?"

"How similar, was Johan also too possessive like Marina?" Richard asked.

"No! Here I was like Marina. But it was a long time ago. Really, really long time ago. It was when we started dating. You see I had a best friend, Aakruti. She was also putting ideas in my head like Johan couldn't be trusted. He is a liar and all."

"Yes, same here. Marina also has her best friends. Especially that Deeksha. She makes me sound like a bad guy all the time. God knows what her problem is with me."

"Anyway, I am not finished with my story yet. So, later I found out that Johan had a best friend. He is a big flirtish guy and is always in friends with benefits kind of a relationship. So that made me worried that my Johan would get bad influenced because of him just like how Marina worries that Deborah... Would be a bad influence on you." She said and he shook his head.

"No! It's not entirely similar. You thought Johan's best friend would spoil him into bad things. But my fiancé thinks I might have sex with Deborah or worse, she might be imagining we already had sex. Either or, she thinks I am a cheater." Richard said and Idhaya agreed.

"Ok, try to prove yourself to her."

"I did try, that dinner was supposed to do that, but it went sideways."

"Johan did prove himself in his own way and ever since it has been working great. Your case is different, so, If you really love her, you'll think of something." She said as she was getting late for her work, she left the cabin.

Days pass by, but things remained the same. Marina was still not talking to Richard. From a simple text to meet in person, everything was a dead end. Things began to worsen up when both of their families found out that their relationship was on a hold. He had never dealt with a situation like this before. The whole of his day was in sour face. Even Deborah's companionship couldn't cheer him up anymore.

After almost two weeks, on 17th October, Deborah came hurriedly into Richard's cabin, got inside and locked the doors. Gazed into his eyes and said.

"Richard, what did you do?"

"What's going on?"

"You don't know it yet. Shit!" Deborah hit her head with her palm.

"What? What happened now to me?"

"You messed up or fucked up, or whatever you can say about it is less."

"What did I do?" Richard sounded calm, but his heartbeat begged the difference. Deborah came closer to her desk and used his office laptop. She logged in her administrator account and showed him his mistake.

"No way, this is not possible. I can't even remember when I did that." Richard was scratching his hairs in distress.

"How could you not remember erasing twenty days of attendance of your candidate? And how could you erase it? You do realize that now your candidates won't get the salary this month." Deborah said and Richard went out of his conscious. His blood pressure began to rise and everything else started to blackout. Darkness was all he could see with his hands shivering in panic. Then he felt a presence of someone, a hand holding his hand firmly. Soft and warm at the same time. His face was frozen at that moment, but then it started to melt as another hand, held it by his cheeks. Then the sound came, low but clear which began to bring light back to his vision. And eventually, he came back into consciousness and saw Deborah holding his palm with one hand face with another. She then very calmly said, "Richard Butthello, you don't have to worry anymore. There's a solution even to this and I am there with you. Relax everything's going to be fine. Ok?" She said and he nodded.

Then she went back to the laptop, log out of her account and told Richard to log in. He logged in and she explained the steps to fix it. But it was something that can't be undone. So what they did was manipulated the data of every other candidate in other departments of their company and converted their paid leave into his candidate's salary. It took many people's paid leave to compensate his loss.

"Is it legitimate, what we are doing right now?" Richard asked.

"Legitimate? This is what a scam looks like Richard. Grow up."

"Scam! What if we get caught? Do we get fired?"

"Unbelievable! You are worried about getting fired while we can go to jail for this." She said and he got scared again.

"Stop worrying Richard, I have done this before. We won't get caught. Ah... Done!" She said and yeah, things got better. Everyone's attendance was scrapped, but somehow, she managed to get them their salary back.

"Huh... Deborah, I don't know how could I thank you."

"How about by stop worrying, What happened now? How's everything going with Marina?"

"What things? We haven't talked since the last dinner."

"I am so sorry about that. It's all my fault isn't it?"

No... of course not. It's all me." Richard said, but she knew that Richard was in this charred of sorrows because of her. They met every day and he always put up a smile on his miserable face. And she always looked at him behind the mask of 'Fine'.

Richard was the only thing close to something called as a friend Deborah had but she couldn't bear the cost of misery Richard was suffering because of her. So, the next evening, Deborah invited Richard for dinner.

He came early that night in terms of leaving soon to home. Looked sick like he was looking these days and just drop dead on the couch. Deborah was taking out the wine, but he rejected it and later he also rejected the company of the cigarette.

"So, you won't drink or smoke or share your problems with me anymore, are we still friends?" She asked a rhetorical question and chuckled but had a dead silence vibe around him.

"That was a joke, Richard. Anyway, how's Marina?" She asked and he glared her.

"She's still not talking? Ok."

Then Deborah took a puff from her cigarette and passed on to Richard.

"I told you I am not smoking." Richard rejected again.

"If you want to fix things, then you need a calm mind, which you don't have right now. Just take a puff and blow out the tension in a smoke." She sounded like a drug dealer which she was acting on purpose but nothing worked with Richard.

"Hey, don't die here, ok? Not in my house."

"Just stop with dry jokes now, please I beg you." Richard said.

"So, tell me. Why won't you even smoke? You aren't giving me a single answer, then how can I help you?"

"I don't need any help. At this point, nothing can save my relationship, everything is gone and I am as good as dead to her or to me as well."

"No, you are not."

"Yes, I am. I even stopped smoking. For real this time to prove myself to her. But I won't get her trust back like this. It isn't even close to enough efforts and I have no clue how to deal with this depression without smoking or drinking. I am fucked!" Richard ended stopping tears coming out of his eyes.

"So, you stopped smoking completely because she hates it." She asked and he smirked.

"And is it working?" She asked and he replied. "Not so much"

"Richard," She said in a low pitch. "I am sorry, I am extremely sorry." She said but he didn't reply.

"Marina hates one more thing. She hates it the most. If you stop it, she might be yours again."

"What are you talking about?" Richard asked and Deborah sounded like a puppy, "Me!"

"Wha... No, I am not going to just ditch our friendship for this."

"What friendship? Some weeks or a month, you think it's even worth for what you had for years." She tried to stay strong.

"But what about you? I can't let you be lonely again."

"I am an independent lady. Practically, I have been alone and strong for so many years. It was nice knowing you so well, but I can easily live without you."

"I know you are lying." Richard said facing away and she tittered.

"Yes, I am, but it's the right thing to do right now." She said and Richard had a sigh of relief.

"Now don't cry in front of me, I don't like crying people. They are so weak and pathetic."

"Yeah, Classic Deborah as always." Richard said and they both chuckled.

"You can leave now, don't need to make this situation more awkward." Deborah said, and he stood up walked by the door. Then he turned around and looked at Deborah like he's looking at her for the first time.

"I am not hugging you goodbye. God, you really make things clichéd." Deborah said, and they both had their last laugh together before he turns around and walks his way out of her life. She was fine with this break up of friendship, at least she was fine for a few hours. Things began to itch when she couldn't sleep at night. Annoyed and irritated for no apparent reason at first. But later at night nearly by 4 am she got really upset for obvious reason and also got cranky because she couldn't sleep cause for that reason.

"No No No... Shut up!" She screamed at the alarm that rang by her head. It was time for her to get ready for her work, but she didn't have any sleep. The alarm won't shut because her hands were twitchy, so she threw it away. Unfortunately, the alarm fell on her 55-inch bedroom led screen shattering its glasses on the ground.

Deborah never really had a morning like this before, such rage and stress that she couldn't control.

"This is not happening to me again. I don't deserve it." She got out of the bed to get coffee. But instead, she decided to choose a cigarette. With each puff, she felt hollow inside.

"No, this isn't fair. I don't want to get depressed." She was talking to herself in such temper that she couldn't even notice her body's movement as she crushes the cigarette and unknowingly burning her finger.

"The FUCK! Ah...! No, this is not right. Why should I always have a sad ending?" Then looked at her burned finger and in deep thoughts, she got a feeling of relief from the pain of and said,

"No! I won't have a sad ending this time, it's your time to now, Richard Butthelo."

Chapter 19

Running its course

Brown eyes like a wild cat yet seducing with her enticing stare. Walked Deborah D'mello in the office and staring sideways at the cabin of Richard Butthelo. His blurry body was visible through the opaque mirror, sitting on his desk with a laptop. Then she walked away straight into her cabin. Dizzy because of insomnia and cranky as she hates everyone around, especially his arch-nemesis now, Mr Butthelo. She opened her laptop as soon as she settled in, Logged in the iHNS corporate server and started writing a mail to the higher executives.

When she was halfway writing the mail, she wondered whether she was doing the right thing or this is just rage and she'll regret this later. She just shut her eyes before typing another word, leant back and took a deep breath, exhaled all her rage and restarted her day there itself getting back to her daily routine.

After almost an hour, she was on her way to smoke a cigarette. While walking, she was passing by Richard's cabin where she kept glancing at but he was nowhere to be found. As she walked looking sideways, she stumbled onto Richard.

"Sorry." She said looking at him being embarrassed a little. She still felt that being apart with each other, there can be an unspoken friendship between them with just a little smile and stares. But that's not what Richard had in mind. He just looked right over her head, without uttering a single word he went on his way while she stood there watching him leave. Every other eye in the office had eyes on them, and that's the moment when Deborah lost it. They both walked in the opposite direction, looking at them was like looking at a double-edged sword. When Richard reached his cabin, a colleague of his asked him.

"Did you guys break up?"

"What? What are you talking about?" Richard was confused as he thought they were talking about his relationship with Marina.

"Just seeing you and Deborah like this. Looks like you both broke up."

"Deb... Deborah!" Richard exclaimed, and a few more ears joined their conversation.

"We were never a thing to break up about. There was nothing ever between us, what are you even talking about?" Richard said.

"Come on, it definitely looks like something was between you two. And it's ok if you both broke up, it happens..."

"Shut up... And get back to your work. You have a deadline to finish." He ended calmly and went inside his cabin.

Deborah on the other side of the sword didn't take things that well. She had a cigarette between her fingers. Lit but not kissed, yet felt like she was puffing it from the inside. Her eyes felt as if she was talking to it. Thinking about how everyone came and went from her life except for the cigarette.

"That's why materialistic things are better, at least they are not fake as people are." Deborah said and threw her cigarette down the street, crushed it on the way back to the office. Every employee, candidates and her colleague watched her walk in blazing anger. Entering her cabin, the first thing she did was opening her laptop and finishing the mail she started writing in the morning.

'Your mail has been sent' came the notification as she leaned back and smirked. The next day in the cafeteria, Richard was walking with his lunch when he sighted Idhaya having lunch with Sheetal. He joined them only to get criticized for something he hadn't even done in real life.

"For the last time I am telling you, we were never in a relationship in the first place. For which you are accusing me of breaking her heart." Richard tried to explain.

"Ok, ok... So, why did you break up?" Sheetal asked and chuckled.

"Idhaya tell her, you know everything."

"She knows everything. She's just messing with you." Idhaya said, Richard made a poker face while Sheetal mumbled, "Sorry."

"Let me guess; you stopped talking to Deborah so you could get Marina's trust back. How's that working for you?" Idhaya asked.

"Hmm... Well, I don't really know. When I went to her house last night and she wouldn't even hug me or even let me touch her at first. Then finally when we started to have a casual talk, I told her that every single bit of a friendship between us was over. We no longer talk or even look at each other. After I was done talking about Deborah, Marina came close to me. So close that our lips almost touched, but then before kissing she lowered down her head and started sniffing my breath. She took a few steps back after that and said. At least you are not smoking anymore, you got that for now. Bye Richard the door is that way. She said and walked into her bedroom, I thought to do the right thing which is not dragging the matter ahead so I said I love you and Left." Richard narrated the whole incident and both Sheetal and Idhaya hit their head with their palms.

"What did I do wrong?" Richard asked.

"This was the moment. You should have followed her to the bedroom and had sex with her. It would have been a perfect makeup sex." Idhaya said.

"No way, I was in the room. Things were really hot between us and by hot I don't mean sexual hot, but there was anger." Richard said.

"Tell me, you are having this quarrel for like a week now, right?"

"More than that"

"That means you haven't had sex too for a long... Time."

"Eh... Yeah... Oh, oh! Yes, you are right. She might be needing it yesterday."

"I am always right." Idhaya said raising her shoulder and folding hands as she leant back.

"But what if she was actually angry, in that case, things could have gone sideways."

"Well maybe, I don't have experience of such fights. Johan and I always have small fights, and all our solution lies in our bedroom." She said blushing.

"Ok... Great, now I just have to come up with another plan to make her believe that Deborah means nothing to me."

"Good luck with that." Idhaya said and left with her friend and in a moment even Richard went to work.

Days passed, by with things began to get better in his life. Turns out Idhaya was right as the first thing Richard did after the office was makeup sex with Marina. They were apart for more than three weeks, but when they got together they became inseparable. Eventually, she gave him the keys to her apartment.

Almost after a week of November, Richard was full of spirit all the time. As he was on the way to another department, he saw Idhaya standing amidst of dreadful vibes. She kept glaring the empty glass of coffee. The way she sat felt like she was frozen that way for a while.

"Idhaya! You here?" He said, shaking her shoulder.

"Oh! Hi Richard." She said in a gloomy voice as she left her space of silence.

"You don't look so good, are you sick?" Richard asked.

"No, I am fine. It's just that I didn't have much sleep for a few days." She said.

"You used to be the happiest soul out here, now look at you. Something is definitely wrong with you, and I won't leave until you share it."

"It's nothing, just workload and deadlines."

"Is it Johan?" Richard asked, and she didn't utter a word, but just shook her head.

"It is Johan then. So, make up sex isn't working anymore?" Richard tried to lighten her mood, but things don't work out well.

"Ok, it's fine if you don't want to talk to me, but watching you I have learned that everything's going to get better in time."

"I really wish that happens. By the way, what makes you come here on this side of the company?"

"I was looking for you. Tell you the good news, next year in January I am getting married."

"Are you serious? Are you freaking serious! But things weren't going so well with you too and now you are getting married!" She was out of her excitement level and that did lighten up her mood. After a good talk, Richard went back to his cabin only to discover that he is screwed. All his dreams, ambitions and marriage planning got standstill when he saw the mail. It didn't even take him a second to realize who was behind this.

"Deborah!" Richard called out her name as he entered her cabin, hyperventilating.

"Come in." Deborah appeared oblivious. Richard walked closer to her desk breathing heavily.

He was glaring her, but she was busy on her laptop.

"Have a seat." She said calmly. He stared at the chair, then raised a finger at her, but before saying a word he sat down.

"You did this." Richard accused her.

"I did what?" She kept her eyes and fingers busy with her laptop.

"Stop hiding and face me, tell me the trut..." As he was speaking, she slammed her laptop and interrupted.

"At least tell me, what did I do?" She asked in slow pitch.

"I am getting fired. They haven't given me the reason yet, but I think I know who's behind this. Tell me, why did you do this?" He talked in agony with rage. Deborah stood up and walked towards the glass window, looking out at the sky she said.

"Richard Butthelo, all this time when we were so-called Friends I ignored my role to the job as manager and I kept protecting you from getting drowned, remember?" She said and his eyes popped out.

"No! You can't do that. You wouldn't do... Hey, you help me do that. That scam is not only my fault, but also yours too. We did it." Richard said.

"You know, the first thing I did when we went separate ways? I started doing my job more seriously. Unlike you, I can't let my personal feelings affect me while doing my work.

So when I looked at the main server and checked everything in detail. I found out that a lot of our employees paid leaves were transferred and converted to your candidate's salary. This was wrong, so I had to put up a mail and explain the ones above us what's wro..."

"Just stop... Stop with this act. It's not just me, but you too. I didn't know anything about it. You helped me with the scam so in a way you are my partner in this crime. If I get fired, you do too." Richard said, raising up from his seat.

"Oh really, who is going to believe you. How are you going to prove it anyway?" Deborah asked, walking up to him.

"I would find a way to and prove that you wer..."

"Remember, while cleaning your mess I logged out of my account and let you login before doing the dirty work. That's how, I am safe, always have been safe." Deborah smirked.

"No... I don't believe this. How could you do this? I thought we were friends." Richard said.

"I did it when we no longer were friends."

"Not that time, but you were always playing safe, just pretending to trust me. You logged out and let me login so you can come out clean." Richard said.

"I always play safe. It's just a part of my reflex."

"It's not just about playing safe, friends always stayed together. The situation doesn't matter, we give our whole self, despite what the outcomes are. I don't want you to be stuck with me, but it turns out, you never really were my friend."

"Just a few days are left for you in this company. Do you want to spend those times fighting with me? Just go out of this cabin. Talk to your friends and just admire every inch of the interior here while you can. But whatever you do, just don't come up here with your despised face." She said folding her hands. Richard walked towards the door. Just when he was about to leave, he smiled and said.

"I am getting married soon, at least I would always have a shoulder to cry on whenever I fail. And somehow, this doesn't look like I have failed. Maybe this is what my destiny is. Being in a place where I could never see your face again. And with you gone completely out of my life, Marina would never even have a thought about you getting stuck with me. God! This is such a relief. Thank you." Richard said and left the room. Deborah stayed casual with the feeling of losing. It wasn't friendship, but self-esteem that she lost that day.

Chapter 20

Checkmate... or is it?

"When was the last time you felt love?"

Deborah asked as she removed her specs and wiped the raindrops on it with a towel. She wore it back and pushed her ponytail hairs behind her shoulder.

"I am in love now."

Richard replied shaping his moustache with his fingers as he steps down the stairs.

"That's not what I meant. I asked when was the last time you felt love?"

Deborah asked again as she raised her blue umbrella and opened it standing under a street lamp. The raindrops falling upon her umbrella sparkled under the pale-yellow street light in the darkest night.

"What's the difference in being in love and feeling love?"

Richard said and wore his black raincoat above his black shirt. He raised his hands sheltering his face as the water from Deborah's umbrella bounced back at Richard when she turned on him.

"You are never going to know what real love is because you are never going to be able to love again."

Deborah said, her face cold as frozen crystal, so fragile. Then she walked with the wind while he walked against it in the shimmering rain.

Long time ago, Present day at the office. Eyes in flames, the rest of the face expressionless. Breath slow and sound with fingers tapping the keyboard rough. Then a lady enters the cabin, looking at Richard says.

"Is everyone angry out here these days?" Said Idhaya and sat on the chair.

"I am sorry, I am not angry, it's just... You know what it is with everything that's cracking me open." Richard said shutting his laptop down.

"Everything's supposed to crack up sometime or the other." Idhaya said smiling.

"You are smiling, wow! Great to have you back." Richard said.

"Yeah, well, that's the very thing why I am here now. I am back, but I am going." Idhaya shrugged.

"You are resigning?" Richard asked.

"No, I am not going forever... Just for a while, on a break..."

"Is everything really alright with Johan?"

"Rich... My life is lost somewhere between dream and love, and I know I can't find my answer here. I won't!" Idhaya

145

said then getting her hands down on the desk, she continued, "I am going out for like a week. Somewhere but Mumbai, I love it here, but I need to know who I am? And the only way to find it out is by being what I am." Idhaya ended smiling.

"So, are you going to Pune?" Richard asked.

"Ah... Yeah, maybe." Idhaya nodded.

"Great have fun."

"Yeah... About that... I am not getting any leave. You gotta help me out."

"What...? I can't give you a leave. It's not in my hands." Richard explained.

"I am not asking you to sanction my leave. You are a team leader; try out with your colleagues. Come on, you can help a friend out, right?" She requested.

"Yes, I will be talking to Shree. After all, he is the head above us all. I will definitely try for you."

"Thank you so much Richard and looking forward to being at your wedding."

"Oh, you have to be there. Come back soon from Pune."

"Yes, from Pune, bye." Idhaya said, smiling her way out.

After she was gone, Richard was back on his laptop. The mail from the company stating he has less than three weeks in this company. Staring at the screen, trying to find out if there's any solution, a way out of it. Angry and frustrated, Richard walked out of his room. He went to TL Shree's cabin and spilt out the beans.

"Damn, your little fights had paid off really bad." Shree said in low pitch.

"How's this my fault...? Ok, yes, most of it is my fault. But is there a way out?" Richard begged.

"I don't know, maybe. How did the meeting go?"

"What meeting?"

"You didn't have the board meeting yet. Be prepared for it." Shree warned him while he hid his head in his palm. Then he looked up to him and asked.

"You were dating... Or whatever that was with Deborah. Did she ever mention anything about me, or you saw her mailing a complain?"

"Richard, we just had sex and that's all. Sure, it was freaky and great, but that's it. Damn, she is a creature in be..."

"Shree, seriously!" Richard exclaimed.

"Sorry, I forget you hate her." Shree said and added, "Damn, she fucked you better than me, how ironic."

"Do you think I am in a mood to laugh?" Richard said and his dead poker face answered the question himself.

"Ok, just so you know, we haven't been meeting for a long while now. So, I thought maybe it ran its course." Shree said.

"How can I save myself?" Richard asked.

"Yeah, that. Well, only she can save you now." Shree replied.

"What?" Richard was shocked.

"If she takes back her complaint stating that it was a mistake or she made a false allegation then you can be saved."

"Is that possible?"

"Only if the investigation hasn't started yet, but she wouldn't do it even in a million years."

"Yes, of course, she won't. Mother of all bitches."

"Not just hate, if she does that then that will affect her position at the office, which took her so long to build." Shree said and he just kept his head down the desk.

"Richard, try to relax. You look pathetic and lost. This won't solve anything. Also, I heard you are getting married, right?"

"Yes, Married. That's the biggest deal of all." He said waking up, "Imagine how it would sound like, getting married being jobless. Since the moment that thought struck my mind, I haven't been in a normal state again."

"When are you getting married?"

"January, mostly."

"You might find a new job till then. It's November now. We still have two mont... Ok, that's too less."

"Yes... way too less. Also, who will hire someone who is fired already." Richard said and they kept on talking, trying to find out a solution that they never could. Richard even talked about his friend Idhaya's request. And at the end of the day was the meeting between the heads, HR, manager and team leader Richard. It was the most unpleasant 45 minutes of Richard's life. The manager, Deborah D'mello seemed to be pleased by that. But her face didn't say a thing as she stayed neutral in all the discussion. Sure, her eyes said how satisfying it was to watch Richard fall down the pit. She kept staring him as his head lowered down and down in abyss. Then all of a sudden, Richard felt something. He raised his head straight up, made eye contact with Deborah. Though she always stayed strong, she wasn't ready for his glare at the moment and thus she faced away to the clock. Richard then turned his head to the heads and said,

"I only have one proposal to make."

"Go ahead." One of the heads said.

"I am agreeing to all the terms given to me for which I am accused of, but my only request is, instead of firing me, let me resign. The terms remain the same, and I will never be a part of this company, but at least, this would help me have a sustainable future." Richard begged and the heads began to discuss.

"No, this isn't the company's policy." Deborah spoke for the first time in 45 minutes interrupting the discussion.

"I understand Ms D'mello, but I have put up my proposal to the heads as a request. And willingly I am ready to accept whatever their decision is, as it's their own decision." Richard said slowly but audible enough, glaring straight into her eyes. Even her eyes were fixed on him as her mouth opens a bit in shock when she heard the solution.

"We will see to your request; the meeting is adjourned."

Later on, he was on his way to Marina's house, his new home. While riding, his phone vibrated in his pocket. He parked aside and checked the notification. Eventually, the board ended up their discussion, and he achieved a small victory. His resignation got approved and instead of 3 weeks, in two weeks he will be kicking himself out.

Happy was Richard, although it was a weird time to be happy as he was going to be jobless. But he felt it was the right moment of his life. The next thing Richard did was going to a gift shop. At Marina's place, when she opened the door, she was surprised to see a big flower bouquet held by a man whose face was covered by it.

"May I come in my love?" Richard said and added, "This thing is freaking heavy."

"This is so beautiful!" Marina's cheeks blushed red. He kept the bouquet aside and lifted her to the couch.

"You look extremely happy today."

"Oh, I am more than that." Richard said, biting her shirt with his lips and he slips down his hands in her shorts. Within a minute she was in her bra and panty while she struggled just to remove his shirt. Soon, when she finally managed to remove his shirt, his mouth was over her dry body, removing the bra by biting it off and his hands under her pants.

Then, as his pants and underpants were also off while her green panty was below her thighs, rubbing his penis on her vagina they then intercourse deep within with their feelings bursting out. They were in the heat of the moment, she rolled above him, riding his penis like a bicycle as his hands couldn't lose the grip of her boobs. Then he raised his body up and bit her nipple and in a seductive voice said.

"Ah... Lets... Get married."

She too replied in a seductive voice as she was in the motion,

"Ah... Ah... We are getting married."

"Yes... Ah... Oh... But wait, I can't wait that long." He said and pushed her back, grabbing her by the ass he pinned her down. And in an erotic fire, he pounded crushing her soul out as she screamed in pleasure. "Oh... Richard!" And he said cuming into her. "We are getting married in a week... Ah... Ah... Oh... Uff..." Then he slows down, and they both stopped banging each other, breathing heavily as Richard laid above Marina's breast she said.

"Oh yeah...! Oh yeah! Oh, in a week... What?" She began to come back to her senses.

"Yeah, there's something happening, so this is the best time." Richard said looking up to her. She pushed him off her naked body, sat straight on the couch and said.

"Richard, Are you alright? You are acting extremely weird."

"Would it still be weird if I say that I, eh... I resigned." He said with a weird smile.

"What?... The fuck! Have you lost your mind? Just doing whatever the fuck you like... Let's just quit work, let's get married. Let's just move to Paris... Is this what you think life is?"

"Honey, calm down." He said again with a weird smile, "Chill, I have a plan... It's."

"Wait." Marina interrupted and stood up, being fully naked she took Richard's shirt, wearing it she went to the kitchen. Pouring out a glass of wine for herself, she came back and after taking a long sip, she said, "Continue."

"Ok, this is how it is. I will find a new job, where I would meet new people, all new faces and no one would be there to interfere in my life again."

"Are you quitting your job because of Deborah?" Marina kept swirling her glass as he went silent for a moment. Then he replied.

"No, for you honey. I know you hate the idea of her even standing in a room with me. I know that it itches you that she is always there close to me and you have to worry about me, I completely understand your concern. So, I have decided to be somewhere else and never make you sad again."

"You are doing this for me?"

"I have always done everything for you." He said kissing her on the head. Then he stood up and went to get dressed.

"Get dressed, we are going to church." Richard said.

"Right now, are we getting married now?" Marina was confused.

"No, but we need to book the date for the wedding."

"Are we really getting married next week? Why not January?"

"Eh... will tell you the answer to that question at the church itself." Richard said wearing a denim jeans and brought a one piece for Marina to wear. Then, within no time, they rushed to the church.

"Alright Richard just stop, I am not getting inside the church unless and until you tell me the reason why we are getting married next week." Marina asked standing near the stairs of the old cathedral church. She wore a black one piece and heels, but her hairs looked messy.

"Yes, it's simple. In two weeks I will be jobless and then I don't know when will I be employed again. I mean I know I will be working soon but if I don't get the job till Jan then how could I marry you. It would be economically difficult and also sounds really weird to marry a jobless man." He said then held her hands and pulled her to walk up the stairs. But she stopped him and said,

"That made some sense, not much and I have a gut feeling that this is a bad idea."

"You want to get married to me, right?" Richard asked.

"Of course, yes, but think about inviting everyone. We can't do that in a week. And my wedding dress, your tuxedo, the hotel for the reception, the food. Oh God, it's so much pressure. We can't do it in a week." Her face stressed the situation.

"Marina! We can. The reception at the hotel, we don't need it. We'll do it over here at the church's place like most people do. And there are plenty of caterers so nothing to worry about the food. Then the dress, from a very long time I have looked a dress for your wedding and you will be wearing that. I have even looked for my tuxedo so even that's ready. Let's just book the church and get married next week." Richard said in excitement and a smile that Marina can't say no to.

"Ok, let's get married." She tried to smile being pressurized.

Inside at the church office, as they were looking for the dates the priest said that only one day is available, six days from then that is 20 November.

"Richard, the date is perfect let's do it." She was finally happy.

"Yes, November 20 it is." He said and took the pen to sign it, but before the ink touched the paper Richard froze. He felt as if the time has frozen along with him because he got struck by the thoughts of reality at once.

"What the hell am I doing? No! This isn't how I planned. I love her, why am I doing this to her? Why am I rushing lik..." As he was in his world of thoughts Marina shook his shoulder and said.

"Richard, is everything ok?"

"Yes, the pen was not working." And he signed the form and said, "Hey, it worked." Quite an awkward situation, it was over there, but he managed to overlook it. The next day he went to the office, jolly and fresh. As he entered his floor starting from the first person he met he said. "Hi, Priya... Right?"

"Yes." She replied.

"I am Richard."

"Ok?"

"Anyway, 20th November is my wedding date. Don't forget to come." He said inviting her and later on every other member in the office. It didn't matter for Richard whether he knows them or not, but if they were in the office, he invited them there itself. Everyone was sort of confused, but there was free food for them so nobody bothered much. Most of his time in the office got spent on talking to every face and inviting them to his wedding. He even went to Idhaya's department, but couldn't find her that day so he invited Sheetal and Daniya too. Everyone except for one cabin, except for one person. He took the next day off and wandered around the shops, finding a wedding dress for his bride and a tuxedo for himself, the groom.

Even after being a rushed decision, his choice turned out to be perfect as she loved the gown Richard brought for her. Simply beautiful yet exceptionally perfect with the rich elegance it had. Nothing could beat the dress and even his tuxedo looked dull as her dress shined. The next day was another leave for him as he went on searching for a caterer. He was acting like a madman on fire. Rushing here and there. Spending money with no regards, just to get married, as if the world would end after a week.

20th November came the big day. The church bells rang loud with the choir singing the hymns of love as the doors opened and arrived Richard Butthelo and Marina George in the church. Her white gown backless with strings of platinum thread from left to right glittered upon her skin as she walked with two little girls pulling her long dress up, keeping it from touching the ground. The front had transparent lace covering her belly, and flowers patterned white satin covered her breast. And at last, the neck, a beautiful diamond necklace that formed a small heart above her cleavage. The tiara was the final piece of her dress that made her look change from a bride to a princess. As compared to that, Richard wearing a black tuxedo with a rose on his pocket and clean shaved face was no win to her appearance but they both simply looked perfect. The ceremony started and the time came.

"Richard, do you accept Marina as your lawfully wedded wife and promise to be with her in sickness and sorrows?" The Priest asked.

"I do." He replied holding her hands strong.

"Marina, do you take Richard as your lawfully wedded husband and promise to support him as a companion throughout his life?"

"I do." She said with a smile she never had before.

"Does anyone have any objection to take here?" The Priest asked the crowd and they all chuckled.

"I now pronounce you husband and wife. You may kiss the bride!" The priest said and they both kissed each other and the rest of the crowd cheered in happiness.

Later, at the reception, Marina noticed that most of the people from Richard's side were the faces she had never seen before and mostly all were looking young.

"Richard...?" Marina asked.

"Yes, Marina Butthelo." Richard said.

"Where are your relatives? I don't see any of the people you showed me before. Who are these people?"

"Oh! They are my office friends."

"So many? Did you invite everyone from the office and not a single one of your relative?" She asked.

"Ah... Most of them were busy and couldn't make it in such short notice... Hey, Matthew is here."

"He is your brother, not a relative. He has to be here." She said making a poker face.

"Yes." He said chuckling and added, "Frankly, it doesn't matter who is here and who isn't. This day belongs to us and only us." He said and calmed the situation down. At the end of the wedding, they both were leaving in a car after everyone wished them farewell as the tradition. They were on their way to the five-star hotel Richard booked for their wedding night. As they were in the car Richard received a mail, it was for an interview for another company he applied for. Then he just looked at Marina and said, "My life is going just perfect, I love you."

"I love you too." She replied with a kiss.

Then they reached the hotel. He took her to the room and said.

"Honey, I need to go out for like 20 minutes, but I will be back soon." Richard went out in his tuxedo and walked towards the building next to the hotel. Got inside the building and stood outside the door on the 14th floor. Rang the bell. The door opened, he said with a crooked smile.

"Hello, Deborah."

"Richard... What are you doing here?" She said as she stood there holding a glass of wine in her hand. She wore a white loose top hanging out her shoulder and navy-blue pant.

"Aren't you going to wish me congratulation?" Richard asked with a smile.

"For what?"

"Oh, you are going to act. Oh well, I got married today. With the love of my life. I am married to Marina Butthelo. Yeah, she is a Butthelo now because she is my wife."

"Oh... Congratulation then." She said like she didn't care or maybe deep within, she really didn't care. Then the timer on the oven went off, and she walked away from the door to turn it off.

"Wait, what? You really didn't know it was my wedding today?" Richard was confused.

"You never told me so how could I know?" Deborah said as she comes back to the door.

I invited everyone from the office, everyone except you. How could you not know that?" He said slowly with the tone of anger in him.

"On the contrary, I don't talk to anyone in the office. I hate everyone. So again I say, how could I even notice?" She said and smirked.

"You are lying, eh... you should have known. I wanted you to feel left out of the party." He whispered.

"Well Richard, I always isolate myself from every party. So yeah, you did me a favour." She smiled.

"The fuck... no wait." He said taking his phone out and showed her the mail, "Look at this, I am going for an interview soon. You successfully got me out of the company, but my life didn't end. I will rebuild it."

"Good for you."

"Stop it... What the hell, I won this. I earned this victory. You lost in your pathetic, lonely world like you always do. You can't even kick me out of the company because I quit myself. I am the winner here who has everything not you, Ms D'mello." Richard was in raging hate, but Deborah just chuckled as she walked back to keep the glass of wine on the table.

"You won? Really? Do you even feel like a winner?" Deborah asked with a smile that could kill a thousand dreams.

"Eh... What?" He said with a heavy breath.

"Richard, look at yourself. Look how terrible you sound. You got married in what, like, a week? Just so you could invite everyone in the office except me. The wedding, which was supposed to happen with all the planning along with all your close people ended up being a wedding with a bunch of office people whom even I don't talk to. You rushed it so much and you got married so early, not for the love you have for Marian but for the hate you had for me. So... it turns out that you dedicated the best day of your life, to me!" She said with the real smile of victory while he was numb and speechless.

"The cherry on top was the part where you resigned. I wanted you to get the fuck out of my office, as soon as possible. Yet I had three weeks to watch your poor face, even after being fired. But with your resignation, all I have to be you is for two weeks. Of which only one week is left. How much more my life could go perfect?"

The word perfect made Richard's heart cry in sorrow.

"Thank you, Richard. I feel really honoured for you are screwing your life up for me. So here, I am the winner!" She said, picking and raising her wine glass up as a toast.

"No, you can't win. This isn't fair." He said getting inside the house.

"What are you doing?" Deborah asked as her smile began to disappear.

"This wasn't a fair game, not yet." He said, pulling up a chair to the table. Sitting on the chair he kept his hands above the table and said.

"You want to win? Then let's play a real game." Richard said.

"What do you have in mind?" Deborah asked.

"Bring out the chess." He said, staring at her. "Very well." She smirked. Then she took out the chess from the shelf, put it on the table. Set it up and asked.

"You really want to play chess with me in your wedding night? Wouldn't the bride be waiting for you?"

"It's fine, our hotel is right there. She can wait."

"That hotel, by my house?" She said and mumbled, "So much dedication." Hearing that he made a poker face and continued.

"If I lose, I accept my failure and will never show my poor face again. But if I win, you will make sure to use all the power you have and take me back to iHNS Pvt. Ltd. back at my post."

"You are too dreamy, that's never gonna..."

"It can happen, I know it can. And I also know that it would affect your position in the company." He said confidently.

"I accept the challenge." She said staring at him fearlessly.

"Alright, shall we begin? Richard said and the game started.

Richard's moves were way better than the last time he played chess with her. It indeed improved and all the time spent on the chess class paid off. He was playing equally good and sometimes even better than Deborah. As she lost her Knight, queen and three pawns while Richard only lost a bishop and two pawns, Deborah said.

"Lucky for you today, wine is in my head and you have the upper hand."

"You can't say that."

"Why? That's the only thing that is making you win this game, so congrats."

"No! You can't do this again. I worked my ass off for this. You cannot below me like this." He said and stood up. Walked up to the kitchen and brought the bottle of wine back.

"What are you doing now, Richie?"

"New rule, this is going to be a fair game. So, whenever a player's piece dies, he or she has to take a sip. That's how the real winner will come out."

"Agreed!" She exclaimed and the game continued.

Deborah took out his pawn with a knight who was guarding his queen. So, Richard took a sip. Then staring at Deborah into the eyes Richard raised his left eyebrow and took out her knight with that queen and then she took a sip. Then she took his queen with her pawn and Richard took a long sip from the bottle. Then Richard took out her pawn with his rock which was guarding her king and he said, "Check."

She took a long sip and said, "Not a checkmate yet." And continued the game. Richard's phone rang which was lying on the ground. Before he could reach out to pick it up, the call got cancelled and the voice mail began to play, a worried voice that said,

"Mr Richard Butthelo, this is Johan, Idhaya's fiancé. I am really sorry to disturb by calling you so early in the morning, but my fiancé, Idhaya. She is not home. She left for someplace I don't know about. This is a serious situation so please respond back as soon as you get this call. Please, Mr Butthelo." Richard finally leaned down and picked it up from the floor, he was feeling too dizzy to use the phone properly. Also, the sunrays blocked his eyesight, so he kept his phone down. He got back up on the bed and suddenly realized something was strange, as he was nude in a bedroom he was never in before. He turned around and his heart stopped, as he saw a naked body, half covered with a blanket while her boobs visible. The lady gently opened her sleepy eyes. There laid bare naked Richard Butthelo next to her, Deborah D'mello. Both under one blanket, close to each other. It took them a moment to grab hold of the reality and to let it sink in. Then their hearts began to pump up hard with heavy breathing, as they looked into each other's eyes popping out and finally realize the fuck they just did.

To be continued...